THANATOS: HIS TEMPTATION

STEEL CHARIOTS, MC BOOK THREE

E. ADAMSON

KNOX
PUBLISHING

Thanatos: His Temptation

Publisher: Knox Publishing

Cover Design: Charli Childs

Editing: Amy Briggs, Knox Publishing

Formatting: E.C. Land, Knox Publishing

Proofreading: Rebecca Vazquez, Knox Publishing

❀ Created with Vellum

To the readers who keep coming back for more, thank you. Without the readers, a writer would have nothing to look forward to. You are my encouragement and my inspiration to keep going.

ACKNOWLEDGMENTS

It's been a long road to get this far, but I've had a lot of help and encouragement along the way and am so thankful for that. Thanks so much to Elizabeth Knox and everyone at Knox Publishing for helping me bring my dreams to life, they have all been wonderful. From the editing to the proofing, to the ones who made the amazing cover. You are all awesome!

CONTENTS

CHAPTER ONE

Thanatos was feeling exasperated as he stomped down the busy sidewalk, making mortals scatter like ants at the fierce glare on his face. Was there a reason for his irritability? Yes, and his name was Zeus. Thanatos wasn't much for words and never said much, but he was so close to telling Zeus off.

Why had they even begun this stupid role-play thing in the first place? Sure, Zeus had explained how role-plays were computer games of some sort. He'd expounded about how in these games, people assume a character in a fictional world and go on adventures and how it had caught his eye. He'd droned on, describing his plans to put a personal twist of his own on it and theoretically make it more interesting for the other gods.

At this point, Thanatos thought Zeus should have

created his own virtual world to play in instead of dragging the rest of them into the mortal world on a whim.

Aren't we a bit old to be playing such childish games?

Thanatos snorted with derision because they were pretending to be in a motorcycle club called Steel Chariots, MC. Not only that, but Zeus, in all his wisdom, had opened a mechanic's garage and an auto-body repair shop. Evidently, in Zeus's mind, this was how they would appear to be a legitimate MC and make money at the same time.

We're gods. Why would we even need mortal money? He snorted again, causing the mortal heading his way to give him a startled look and scurry away quickly.

An auto-body shop that does a bit of mechanic work on the side was what Zeus came up with as the perfect job for us to do. Zeus called it our cover and said it gives us a reason to be in this town. Thanatos grunted irritably. *We are gods; we know little about these contraptions the mortals call automobiles, at least I don't. Why couldn't we just be a bunch of bored rich men in a club? Not only that, but why must it be me who must play the "mechanic" in his garage? Stupid Zeus. I suppose he thinks because mortals' perception of me is that I'm big and scary, it's best to hide me away in his filthy garage. Maybe he feels a little grease on my hands and face will make me less scary. Yes, I agreed to come and be in his club, but I believe I would have thought twice about*

doing it if I'd genuinely known what all it would all entail.
He shook his head *as if I honestly had any say in it once Zeus asked.*

Today they needed parts for some weirdly shaped little car called a Nissan Cube. To Thanatos, it looked somewhat like a box on wheels, and he hadn't been able to stop himself from staring at the oddity of it. He knew it wasn't something he would ever drive, but Eros had found it cute. Anyway, Zeus had sent him and Apollo off to locate the part needed for it at Cotter's Auto Parts, the parts store they used regularly. Why they couldn't have had it delivered to the garage today the way they always did, he would never know.

Lost as he was in his maddening thoughts and testiness, he never saw the petite woman as she walked out of a store in front of him. Until, of course, he slammed into her and almost knocked her down.

"Oh!" the woman yelped. Her arms started wind-milling as she tried to stop herself from falling.

"I am so sorry, miss, I didn't realize anyone was coming out the door," Thanatos murmured as softly as he could in his naturally gruff voice. He caught her elbows to keep her from hitting the ground as he continued speaking softly, hoping not to scare her. "I should have been paying better attention to my surroundings."

The woman turned her large green eyes up from

where they were level with the top of his rib cage to meet his dark ones.

Thanatos eyed her beautiful face as he waited to see what her response to him would be. There were many ways mortals reacted to him, and one was a squeak of fear, which usually came from the women. The squeak was usually preceded by a noticeable body shiver as a feeling of cold moved over them. He'd been told when it happened it would leave what mortals called chill bumps behind on their skin and tended to raise their body hair up on end. Then there was the gasp of fear before they practically ran from him. They all ran from him, men and women, old and young alike. He made all of them too uncomfortable to stay in his presence long.

Early in life, he's learned that even though certain mortals didn't feel the "cold of death," his features were enough to intimidate most of them.

All the gods were tall, but he was even taller, standing a couple of inches over seven feet. He was also more muscular than most of them. His shoulders were broad, his biceps and chest muscles large and defined as if he spent a lot of time at the gym working out. Even though he was as handsome as the other gods, he'd heard multiple times how his perpetual frown, along with his size, turned people off. Some even said he had a dark aura. Which, when he'd thought about it, it had made sense to him. After all, he was the Greek god of death.

None of these things exactly endeared him to the fairer sex, especially mortal women. He honestly didn't intend to come across as angry all the time, and he really could be a gentle soul.

The truth is nobody ever takes the time to get past my intimidating size and see the real me.

However, a sound of fear never came from the petite woman standing in front of him. Neither did she shiver as if she were cold. Instead, she gave him a bright smile which caused his heart to beat fast because of its brilliance.

"It okay. I wasn't paying any attention either. I was digging through my purse for my phone, so I could call my brother and tell him I was ready for him to come to pick me up. I seriously wasn't watching where I was going," she admitted softly.

Thanatos gave her a nod and tried to smile, fearing it was probably more of a grimace than a smile even as he attempted it. Nevertheless, he found the woman beautiful and decided to take the risk of trying to speak to her. So, taking a quick breath for courage, he opened his mouth to say something only to be interrupted before he could by someone yelling his name.

"Skull! There you are, why did you run off and leave me? It's a good thing I knew where you were going, or…" Apollo was ranting as he jogged up to Thanatos. He came to a halt next to Thanatos and paused his rant momentarily. "Oh, I see, you found a pretty lady to talk to."

The woman slowly turned her head toward where Apollo now stood. She tilted her head as she studied him, from the top of his golden-blond head of curls to his black biker boots. Then her gaze moved back up to his face once more.

Thanatos heaved a sigh of frustration. *She'll never look at me again now that she's gotten a good eye-full of golden boy over there.*

"I didn't know you needed me to wait for you, Prophet," Thanatos grumbled in a sarcastic tone, barely remembering to use Apollo's road name. "I thought you were a big boy and could find your way around."

The woman returned her gaze to Thanatos, and he caught her studying his vest.

She nibbled on her lip for a moment before she murmured, "Skull Crusher?"

Thanatos chuckled, drawing her gaze back to his face. "Yes, that's my road name."

"Road name?"

"Mm-hm… Prophet and I are in a motorcycle club, the Steel Chariots, and we have what is called a road name," Thanatos explained.

"I heard a while back a motorcycle club had come to town," the woman said as she nodded. "Why would they call you Skull Crusher though, and why is his name Prophet?"

"Well…" Thanatos began only to pause as he pondered how to answer. He genuinely liked what he saw of her so far, and he wanted to get to know her since she didn't seem scared of him. However, he'd never been good with words.

Thanatos noticed Apollo rolling his eyes, probably because he was taking so long to answer.

"What Skull is trying to say," Apollo began, "and not doing a particularly good job of, is I have a gift for knowing things. Like a prophet of old."

The woman turned her gaze back to Apollo, listening.

"Skull here is our club enforcer and has crushed a few skulls along the way in the name of keeping our club safe," Apollo added with a wink and a grin that showed his dimples. "Therefore, he is Skull Crusher, but we usually just call him Skull."

"Oh," she murmured with a slight nod of understanding.

Thanatos didn't like how she seemed to be taking in Apollo's boyish features. So, he gave the baby-faced god a glare for drawing her attention.

Apollo just smirked and crossed his arms over his

chest as he puffed it out. Not that he had much chest to puff out since he was one of the slimmer gods. He seemed to be saying, "what are you going to do about it?" to Thanatos.

Thanatos wasn't going to be outdone and placed his forefinger under her chin. Gently, he turned her head until she was once more facing him again. Once her gaze locked with his, he asked, "Tell me, darling, what is your name?"

Her face instantly turned pink, but she held his gaze as she whispered, "Andrina."

"Andrina, beautiful name for an even more beautiful woman. Did you know your name means 'daring' in Greek?" Thanatos asked as he trailed his fingertips along her pink cheek. The feel of her soft skin against his rough fingers sent shivers of awareness down his spine.

"Oh, I know because my mom told me, but trust me, I'm about as daring as a newborn kitten," Andrina muttered. Then clearing her throat, she added, "My father was Greek, at least that's what my mom tells us, and we have his last name, Dukakis."

"Dukakis is most assuredly a Greek surname," Apollo murmured from next to them. "You talk as if he isn't around anymore though. If I may ask, why is that?"

"He didn't stick around long enough to see my

brother and me born but went back to Greece. At least, I assume that's what he did," Andrina informed them, sounding unsure as she glanced at Apollo. With her eyes narrowed thoughtfully, she returned her attention to Thanatos and mused, "You two look like you could be Greek though. I think perhaps it's the shape of your eyes and your nose…"

Thanatos nodded slightly at her correct assumption as he told her, "We are."

"Skull, we should go get the part we're here for now before Tank blows a gasket at how long we're taking." Apollo snickered softly, then asked, "Get it? Part, gasket?"

Thanatos felt like growling, and it took all his control to keep his eyes from blazing red in his irritation. He wanted to get to know this lovely mortal standing in front of him, not roam around buying car parts for Zeus. Cutting a glare Apollo's way, he curled his lip in a silent snarl.

"Eh, I'll take that as a no," Apollo huffed.

Thanatos took a deep breath, calming his irritability, saying, "Go get the part, and I'll meet you back at the clubhouse."

"Skull, I don't think…" Apollo began.

Thanatos turned his head so he could glare at the other man. "Did I ask you to think?"

Apollo put his hands up in surrender before turning on his heel and leaving.

Thanatos returned his gaze to Andrina and stated, "I'll take you home if you like."

"Oh, it's okay. I don't want you to get into trouble on my account."

"It won't get me into any trouble. Tank just likes to throw his weight around and pretend we should all be at his beck and call," Thanatos explained. "He needs to learn I am not one of his minions."

Andrina stared deep into his eyes as she breathlessly murmured, "I don't know you, which means I shouldn't be so trusting as to let you take me anywhere. My brother would have a conniption if he knew I was even contemplating letting a stranger take me somewhere. Nevertheless, there is something about you…"

Thanatos held his breath as he waited for her to continue. When she didn't finish her thought, he took a deep breath and, in a tone of voice which brooked no arguments, he stated, "I will take you home."

Andrina's eyes widened momentarily, her pupils slightly dilating as she agreed, "Okay."

Thanatos smirked to himself. *So glyké mou peirasmé, you seem to like it when I show a little dominance over you. I'll have to remember that in case we meet again. And if I have my way, we will meet again, and it will be soon.*

"My motorcycle is around the corner in the large parking lot there," Thanatos told her. He took her hand, encouraged her to turn, and began to walk with her back the way he had come.

Andrina moved along with him, but with a glance up at him, she murmured, "I thought you and Prophet were together."

"We were, but we rode our motorcycles," Thanatos explained. He glanced down at her as he asked, "You aren't scared to ride on one, are you?"

Andrina shook her head. "No, I've never ridden on one, but the thought of it doesn't scare me."

Thanatos smiled and squeezed her hand as he said, "Good."

They spoke no more until they reached his motorcycle. The Harley Davison Fat Boy was big, black, sleek, and low to the ground. It also had a decal of in his true form on it. It was a man dressed all in black, with long dark hair which hid most of his face, glowing red eyes, and black wings. He also held a scythe in his hand that seemed to gleam in the light of the sun. He'd added the scythe just because these modern mortals expected it, and sometimes he did use it, just for the fun of it, but it indeed wasn't necessary.

Andrina stepped forward to run her hand over the shiny metal, pausing when she reached the decal. Slanting her eyes upward to observe him from under her lashes, she said, "I like this much better than if you had a skull on it, which would have made sense given your name."

"Skulls are overrated, for the most part. However, I do have one." Holding out his arm, he pulled his shirt sleeve up to his shoulder. He had a half sleeve of tatts going from his shoulder to his elbow that he'd gotten because he'd heard a lot of bikers had them. Thankfully, they weren't permanent because he hadn't decided if he genuinely liked how they looked or not.

Pointing at the center of his outer upper left arm, he showed her the tattoo of a skull with a pair of crossed scythes behind it, flames in the empty eye sockets. The rest of his tattoo that made up his half sleeve was mostly something he'd seen and had recreated on his arm. It was something called Greek warrior art and mainly consisted of geometric shapes.

Andrina hummed as she took hold of his arm and seemed to take in every detail of the tattoo. Tilting her head so their gazes met once more, she stated, "It suits you, but I don't think I'd want one. I had a friend who tried her best to talk me into going and getting a tattoo with her. She wanted to get a flower, I thought perhaps a dragonfly would be cool, but I chickened out when I saw what all was involved."

"It isn't for everyone."

Andrina let go of his arm and turned back to his

bike. Running her finger over the decal on his bike, she asked, "Is this supposed to be an angel of death?"

Thanatos felt a shiver of need move through him that was almost as strong as when she'd held his arm. It felt as if her fingers were running lightly over his skin instead of the metal of his bike.

He cleared his throat and waited for her to glance up. When she did, his usually deep voice was even deeper timber because of his desire for he when he pronounced, "It's Thanatos, the Greek god of Death, or the personification of death, whichever way you wish to look at it."

"Well, I always thought of him as a god," she murmured, her fingers still moving over the decal. "Although, I don't think too much has been written about him in the mythology books."

Thanatos stepped up behind her. His chest barely brushed against her back as he leaned over to whisper in her ear, "I can tell you all about him if you wish."

"You know that much about him?" Andrina asked, sounding breathless, her body now trembling against his. She glanced over her shoulder to connect her eyes with his.

"I do," Thanatos agreed as he watched her eyes once more dilate.

At precisely that moment, Thanatos knew how Hades and Ares had felt when they had met their match in a mortal woman. Instantaneously, he knew he'd found the one for him, and it pleased him.

Andrina was short, compared to him at least. However, she was probably average for a mortal woman. She was also very curvy with large breasts, wide hips, and plump thighs.

Thanatos had allowed his eyes to roam over those curves more than once because they thrilled him in all the right ways. The thought of moving his hands and mouth over those curves had him feeling aroused and his pants tightening.

Andrina had beautiful long straight brown hair falling to her waist. Along with that, she had prominent green eyes and a pert little nose.

The longer he gazed at her, the stronger the urge to kiss her became, but Thanatos knew it was too soon. So, shaking himself mentally, he quickly moved back from her. He placed his hands on her arms and gently pushed her to the side so that he could mount his motorcycle. Clearing his throat, he motioned to the seat behind him as he suggested, "Perhaps we should get you home now."

Andrina nodded silently, and in a soft voice, she gave him her address before climbing on behind him. He had the motorcycle started with one quick motion, and they were taking off down the road.

CHAPTER TWO

Ten minutes later, Thanatos was swinging into the driveway of a large brick home in a gated community. He raised an eyebrow at the fancy home and knew Andrina's family had plenty of money.

Andrina climbed off from behind him. Once she had both feet flat on the ground, he also got off and took her hand. "Andrina…" He barely got her name out before someone shouted her name.

"Andrina!"

Thanatos bit back a growl at being interrupted and turned to see who had done it. He found a young man who was swiftly making his way toward them with a scowl on his face. As he drew closer, Thanatos saw the resemblance to Andrina and realized this was the brother she had mentioned earlier.

"Kristos, why are you so angry?" Andrina asked once her brother was standing in front of them.

"I was waiting for you to call me, but you never did," Kristos retorted. "Do you know how worried I was?"

"I'm sorry, Kristos, I didn't mean to make you worry," Andrina whispered as she peered down at her feet. "I was going to call you and was digging for my phone to do exactly that when I ran into Crusher and his friend. We got to talking, and I completely forgot about calling you. Then he offered me a ride home…"

Kristos snorted, bringing Andrina's eyes back up to his and causing her to stop speaking. "Crusher?"

Andrina smiled and peered at Thanatos as she said, "Well, technically, it's Skull Crusher, but I don't like the skull part, so I've decided to call him Crusher."

Kristos turned his full attention to Thanatos at her words, his eyes narrowing as they swept over Thanatos from head to toe. Thanatos knew right away the man didn't like him. However, it didn't bother him much because the feeling was mutual.

"A biker," Kristos sneered with disgust. "Thank you for bringing my sister home. You may leave now and forget where you dropped her off."

"Kristos! That's a rude thing to say when Crusher was nice enough to…"

Kristos turned his narrowed gaze toward his sister,

16

which had her sentence trailing off for the second time. "And I thanked him. Andrina. He's a biker, little more than a thug, and you have no business hanging around such trash. He is the kind of people who break in on people like us because we have more than they do."

Thanatos let out a grunt of disgust at the boy's words.

Kristos turned to ask, "What? It's true. You probably live in a rundown clubhouse where you and your biker friends drink cheap beer and screw every girl that crosses your path after snorting a line of drugs."

"You have it all figured out, don't you, little man?" Thanatos murmured in his deep voice, hanging onto his temper by a thread. Stepping closer to Kristos, he watched him tremble even as he lifted his chin belligerently. "I probably have more money than you could ever dream of, I live in a genuinely nice home, and Tank would probably bring the lighting down, frying you to a crisp if he ever caught you talking about his clubhouse in that manner. As far as cheap beer? I never touch the stuff. Drugs? No, I have no interest in them either. Whores? I have no interest in them. Your sister, however? Unlike you, she seems very accepting of those that are different than her. Because of that, I like her, and I think I'd enjoy getting to know her better."

"Stay away from my sister," Kristos snapped, his hands now balled into fists at his side. He then bowed up, puffing his chest out like a banty rooster as if he could intimidate Thanatos.

Thanatos smirked, not intimidated at all by the six feet nothing man in front of him. Instead, he leaned in, and in a gravely yet cocky tone, he insisted, "Not happening."

Hearing Andrina's sharp intake of air, he glanced at her, thinking he might have gone too far in the way he'd treated Kristos. Instead, he found her cheeks pink and a spark of interest in her eyes. Feeling like she would encourage his interest in her, he told her, "I'll find you later, *glyké mou peirasmé*, for I cannot stay away."

Then, climbing back on his motorcycle, Thanatos drove off while he still could.

Andrina stood for a long moment, watching the motorcycle and the man who had captured her attention as he roared off down the street.

"What was that all about Andrina?" Kristos asked coldly.

My sweet temptation, that's what he called me. Andrina sighed dreamily as a slight smile bloomed on her face.

She completely ignored her brother's hard stare as she gazed into the distance, watching the motorcycle slowly fade from her sight. *Crusher is so perfect...*

"Andrina!" Kristos shouted.

"No need to shout, brother," Andrina told him as she finally turned to face him. "I'm standing right here and can hear you perfectly fine."

"Then stop ignoring me," Kristos snarled. "Now, you will not be seeing that man again, do you hear me?"

Taking a deep breath and squaring her shoulders back, she informed him, "Yes, I will be seeing him again. Honestly, Kristos, I think he could become someone incredibly special to me, and I won't give him up because you want to be bossy."

"He's a biker, Andrina, and he doesn't move in the same circles we move in," Kristos continued as if she hadn't spoken.

Andrina turned and headed up the driveway toward the house. Then, over her shoulder, she tossed out, "I don't care."

"You will care when I lock you in your room," Kristos shouted from behind her. When she stopped walking, he added, "I'm your older brother, and it is my job to..."

Andrina turned, throwing her hands up in the air in disgust as she lashed out, loudly arguing, "You are all of ten minutes older than me, my dear twin! I don't usually say much when you become Mr. Bossy, but I'm telling you right now, *butt out!*" She then stalked off and slammed the front door of the house behind her as she entered.

"Kristos? Andrina?" Mom called out from somewhere further into the house.

"It's just me, Mom!" Andrina hollered.

"Stop yelling in the house, please, and come in here. I want you to tell me what is wrong," Mom called back.

Andrina headed for the sitting room and her mom. Walking in, she saw her mom was smiling from where she sat on the couch. *Hopefully, Mom will take my news better than Kristos did.*

Mom patted the seat next to her as she said, "Sit, dear."

Sitting down, Andrina huffed slightly before saying, "Hi, Mom."

Mom chuckled. "Hello, Andrina. Now, would you mind telling me what you and your brother are fighting about this time?"

Andrina chuckled at her mother's words as she laid her head back against the back of the couch and closed her eyes. Indeed, the fighting between her and Kristos was nothing new. They fought most of the time because Kristos thought it was his right as her brother to tell her what she should and shouldn't do. Not wanting to admit that fighting was what they had been doing, she asked, "How do you know we were fighting?"

Mom laughed then and said, "If the yelling coming from outside hadn't clued me in, the front door slamming would have. I also figured your brother was egging for a fight when he stormed out of here a few moments ago like his shirttail was on fire."

"Yeah, I guess that would be a pretty big clue. Although, the slamming door could have been the wind since Kristos left it open," Andrina imparted with a defeated sigh. She truly needed to learn control over her urge to slam doors.

"Mm-hm, it seems to me it would take hurricane-force winds to slam it that hard," Mom declared with another laugh. "So, again, I ask, what were you fighting about?"

"I met a guy today, and he was nice enough to bring me home. Kristos didn't like the bad boy vibes he had going on," Andrina explained as she rolled her head sideways to focus on her mom. Just then, the door slammed a second time, warning them that her brother had arrived.

Kristos walked into the room with a dark scowl on his face as he asked, "Did she tell you, Mother?"

Mom laughed, covering her mouth with her hand

to muffle it when her son's face darkened even more. She cleared her throat, her eyes still twinkling with humor as she replied, "She was just about to."

Kristos threw himself onto the loveseat opposite of the women and crossing his arms; he continued to glare at his sister. He waved his hand around in front of him as he lamented, "Go ahead, Andrina, tell her about the tattooed and pierced, low-life thug that brought you home just now."

Andrina sat up straight and glared right back as she argued, "He may have some tattoos, and one piercing, Kristos, just one! I have more than that…"

"Piercings should be done on the ears, Andrina, not the eyebrow," Kristos interrupted.

"And he is not a low-life thug," Andrina continued as if he hadn't spoken. "He was a genuinely nice man who brought me home even though he didn't have to."

"Low-life thug? Andrina, what kind of people are you associating with these days?" Mom questioned with a mocking gasp. Then, with sparkling eyes, she persisted, "I thought I taught you better than that. Should I be worried?"

Kristos smirked, utterly oblivious to the laughter in his mom's eyes as he mouthed, "I told you so."

"His name is Skull Crusher, or at least that's his road name. He's in the motorcycle club that came to town a while back. The Steel Chariots MC, I believe he called them," Andrina explained, glaring back at him.

"Oh—so, he's a biker?" Mom questioned, with no hint of being irritated by the fact. Instead, a slight smile crossed her face.

Andrina softly answered, "Yes, and a very polite one at that. I ran into him as I was coming out of the boutique today. Anyway, I thought he was charming and handsome. Oh, Mom, you should see him." She fisted her hands against her chest and heaved a heavy sigh. "He's as handsome as a Greek god."

"Why, Andrina, you seem like you are about to swoon," Mom teased, "just look at those rosy cheeks!"

Andrina laughed. "I almost did when I met him."

"Seriously, Mom? You're just going to let go of the fact that this supposedly Greek god handsome and charming man is in a motorcycle club?" Kristos sputtered with disgust. "He's probably a drug user or dealer, or both…"

"Kristos!" Mom scolded. "You do not know the man, so you have no right to be making assumptions like that."

Kristos rolled his eyes as he said, "Please, she doesn't know him either. Besides that, he's in a motorcycle club which probably means he's running from the law half the time because he's running guns, or…"

"From a drug dealer to a gun runner, wow,"

Andrina muttered in disgust. She never knew her brother could be such a snob.

"Kristos, that is a stereotype, and not all clubs are like that. In fact, I'll have you know that back in the day, I owned a motorcycle myself. I even rode with the local motorcycle club in my hometown for a short time," Mom informed him. "My motorcycle was big, black, and loud. A woman on a Harley was what caught the attention of the man who became my husband, your father."

"Oh, well! Since that worked out so well, maybe Andrina *should* date a biker," Kristos griped.

Mom sighed and rubbed her eyes before saying, "Kristos, your father had no choice but to leave us. He didn't want to, but he had to go home to Greece because his father was dying."

"He could have returned for us," Andrina said, siding with her brother on this one. "Or you could have gone with him."

"Children, I loved your father, and he loved me, but the truth is we were both young and stupid," Mom said sadly. "He left, worried for his father, who he loved dearly, not knowing I was pregnant."

"You told him later, though, right?" Andrina questioned softly.

"I tried, Andrina, I did, but he was in Greece, and it

was so far away," Mom whispered, her eyes filling with tears.

"Mom, have you been lying to us about Dad?" Kristos asked as he sat up straight.

Andrina was beginning to feel just as upset. Neither she nor Kristos had heard this story about their father.

"Not exactly," Mom hedged as she rubbed her forehead, appearing slightly nervous. "I just left out a few details because the two of you were too young to understand any of it. Then, by the time you were old enough to have understood, both of you had stopped asking. It was easier just to let sleeping dogs lie."

"I think I speak for both of us when I say we'd like to hear the truth now," Andrina solemnly told her.

Sensing movement, Andrina glanced over to see her brother getting up from his chair. When he joined her and their mom on the couch, Andrina smiled at him, holding out her hand for him to take. Once he had, he gave it a light squeeze before they turned to give their mom their full attention. Their petty argument was on the back burner for now as they showed solidarity to their mom.

"After your father was gone, I found out I was pregnant with the two of you. I was only nineteen and still in college, that's why I didn't go with him. He felt my education was important and as bad off as his father was, we honestly didn't think he'd be gone long," Mom told them as a few tears escaped her eyes. She wiped at them with a shaking hand and took a deep breath. "I tried to find your father, to find a number to reach him when I realized I was pregnant. Honestly, I didn't even really know where to start because all I had was his father's name, and it was a common one. Greece was a long way off, so making an international call was expensive, and I had truly little money, but I tried.

"Your father told me before he left that he wanted to marry me, and I said yes. So, we decided to marry at the courthouse only two days before he left. We loved each other so much, and he thought marrying me would give me comfort while he was gone, and it did for a while until I realized I was pregnant. That's when I got scared because I was alone at eighteen with my husband away in a foreign country.

"When I was unable to locate him, I did the best I could and hoped he would be home soon. Months passed, and he didn't come home though, and it caused me so much stress which in turn caused complications in my carrying the two of you," Mom murmured sadly. She then sighed as she continued, "You need to understand, I had no one to depend on, I had to quit school, and I barely survived having to work a full-time job while I was pregnant. It was a real struggle to make ends meet, and I had to depend on the charity of others a lot of the time."

"Oh, Mom," Andrina whispered, taking her mom's hand in hers.

Mom squeezed her hand and gave her a gentle smile. "The two of you were about six months old when I received a letter from a lawyer." Mom cleared her throat, wiped away a few tears, then continued, "It was from your father's family lawyer, and it told me how I was now the widow of Kristopher Dukakis and that I had inherited a large sum of money. He told me how sorry he was for my loss and that he needed me to call him. He needed to know details only I could give him, which would enable him to send me money."

"Dead? He's been dead all this time?" Kristos asked, "We thought he just left you."

"I know, but I didn't know how to tell you. I think in the back of my mind, and in my heart, I still believe your father lives, even now. I suppose the reason for it is because I never saw his body laid to rest," Mom whispered, tears rolling down her face heavier than before. She stopped talking then to take a deep breath and clear her throat.

Andrina rubbed the back of her hand soothingly as they waited for her to continue.

"Anyway, apparently, he went into his father's home, after laying him to rest, and began the process of selling everything off, so he could return to the States, to me. Unfortunately, Kristopher didn't know about the bad company his father had been keeping, which caused him to get shot in cold blood in his father's home. The lawyer told me that Kristopher had written a will as soon as he had gone home to Greece though, because seeing his father so ill at a young age had made him recognize his mortality. He told his lawyer that he didn't want his wife to be without if something were to happen to him. The lawyer said he believes that Kristopher had a premonition of his death, and that was the true reason for him writing the will."

"Letters? Couldn't you have written letters to each other, stayed in touch?" Andrina asked, trying to understand it all.

"I did, or I tried," Mom admitted. "I must have written the address down wrong because they all came back to me. He may have tried writing to me also, but I had to move out of the house we were renting because of everything that happened, and I stayed in a women's shelter for months. Living there, I had no way to receive mail and was too naive and stupid to think about a post office box since I had no mail coming that would require me to have one. I wouldn't have even received the lawyer's letter if he hadn't contacted the Sheriff's department. They were able to track me down using my name," Mom admitted, shame-faced.

Kristos sat back with a grunt and a sigh as he said, "Wow, all this time, I thought he just couldn't be bothered with us, maybe even had another family somewhere; instead, he was dead. I suppose we should have asked, but honestly, since I never knew him, it just didn't seem to matter much."

For a long time, the three of them just sat in silence, taking in all that had been discussed.

CHAPTER THREE

Thanatos stood leaning over a car with the hood up. A woman had brought it in that morning for them to fix because it seemingly had a belt squealing, and she wanted it to stop. So, Zeus had informed him it was his job to correct the problem.

As if I have a clue where to even begin solving the issue. The woman said it needed the belt replaced. Why does an automobile need a belt? It wears no pants.

He rubbed his thumb over his chin as he continued to stare at the engine. Thanatos had to wonder why he was even still there pretending to be something he wasn't when he could be relaxing at home. Muttering in Greek under his breath, he scowled and poked his finger at a long, slender, rubber thing, wondering if it might be a belt.

"Skull, dude, what was that about earlier?"

Thanatos turned his head to glare at Apollo as he walked over to him. Flashing his red eyes, he snarled, "Prophet, don't call me dude ever again."

Apollo chuckled, seemingly unbothered by the sour mood Thanatos had been in all day. Shrugging, he asked, "What was up with the mortal female?"

Thanatos turned to once more stare at the car engine as he muttered, "Nothing."

Apollo laughed loudly, drawing the other mortals' attention before turning to sit on the front of the car and crossing his arms. Gazing at Thanatos, he hummed, then in Greek, he murmured, "It didn't seem like nothing to me. You know, you should stay away from the mortal chicks, nothing but trouble."

"No, not this one," Thanatos argued back in Greek.

Apollo huffed out a puff of air in irritation at Thanatos' obtuseness. Then, still speaking Greek and almost in a whine, he implored, "Come on, Thanatos, you can't fall for this girl. I know she was giving you the eye, but we're gods; that's what mortal women do. They flirt and flutter around us, and we take what they offer. Then we leave them behind for greener pastures."

Thanatos gave Apollo his full attention as he straightened to his maximum height of seven feet, two inches. Glaring, he answered, "Mortal women might do that around you, but not me. Most women fear me,

Apollo, you know that. However, this one didn't. Instead, she smiled at me."

"So, you're going to throw your life away because a chick smiled at you?" Apollo asked in an incredulous tone, now in English.

"No, I'm going to throw my life away because I think she might just be the one for me," Thanatos decisively informed Apollo. Turning back to stare at the car engine again, he solemnly admitted, "I felt different with her than I've ever felt before in my long life, and I liked it."

"No, Thanatos, I'm begging you!" Apollo pleaded. "Don't do this."

Thanatos turned his entire being toward Apollo and saw a very un-god like expression on his face. It was a face that held a look of... fear? Confused, he asked, "Why? What is the big deal?"

Apollo sighed, dropping his head as he once more switched to Greek to mutter, "Two of the grumpiest, snarliest, meanest, and darkest of the gods, Hades and Ares, have fallen for mortal women. They are disgustingly happy with those females. If death himself falls for a mortal woman, the rest of us might as well give up because we stand no chance of holding out!"

Thanatos stared at the god, puzzled as to why this was a bad thing. He began to think, *Hades and Ares, for the first time in an exceptionally long time, are happy. They are so blissful that they could almost take over Eros's job of putting couples together on Valentine's Day and do an excellent job of it. What's wrong with that? What's wrong with them being content?* Curious as to what the big deal was, he asked, "What is wrong with them being happy?"

Apollo lifted his gaze to focus on Thanatos. His face was now expressionless as he answered, "Nothing, I just don't want to fall into the love trap."

"So, don't fall," Thanatos stated as he crossed his arms and glared. "No one is forcing you to find a woman and fall in love, but don't try to deny me my happiness because it isn't what you want."

"True, nobody is forcing me, but love seems to float around this place like a highly contagious virus which has been let loose, and I don't want to catch it!" Apollo yelled in Greek as he backed away from Thanatos. Switching back to English, he concluded by saying, "So, stay away from me."

Thanatos shook his head. He had to wonder if the heat from the sun had become too much for Apollo as he watched him walk off. Contagious virus indeed!

"What was that all about?"

Thanatos glanced over at the car to his right. Just then, a man rolled out from under the car with a part in his hand.

"Whatever language he was speaking was unknown to me."

"It was Greek." Thanatos sighed, thankful he and Apollo had been talking low and mostly in Greek. He'd forgotten the man was even there.

"Ah," the man said. "And the reason he was yelling at the top of his lungs for you to stay away from him? That will be hard to do since you work and ride together."

Apollo had yelled the last of it in English, and it was enough to raise the mortal's curiosity. So, quickly thinking of how he could explain Apollo's behavior, Thanatos said, "We met a woman while we were out earlier. He's used to the women practically falling all over him because of his handsome face , and I think it shocked him when she seemed more interested in me. So, maybe he's just jealous of that, I don't know."

"So, he's lashing out," the mortal man said knowingly. "My brother was always that way when we were younger. He's married now, though, so he leaves the girls I date alone, although I haven't dated in a long while. Anyway, better keep an eye on him because my brother always seemed to know when I'd grown attached to a girl, and that's when he'd strike, trying to steal her away."

Thanatos was now curious, so he asked, "What did you do when he did that to you?"

The mortal stood up and shrugged as he wiped his hands. "There wasn't much I could do, not really. I always figured if the girl genuinely cared about me, she wouldn't have let her eyes stray to him in the first place. Maybe he did me a favor flirting with those girls because I knew they didn't genuinely care about me if they started chasing after my brother. One day though, I'll find a sweet girl that will see me and only me. That's what I'm waiting for."

"Well, I hope you find her, my friend," Thanatos murmured.

With a shrug, the mortal walked over to the toolbox and began hunting through it.

Thanatos turned away to stare down at the engine once more, deep in thought. He began humming under his breath as he thought about the mortal's words and about how he'd first met Andrina. She hadn't given Apollo more than a brief once over. *Is that a sign that she holds no interest in him? Is she genuinely interested enough in me to overlook Apollo's beauty? I believe it just might be the case, and I am convinced she is the one for me because of it.*

The mortal returned, a wrench in hand, and chuckling, which brought Thanatos' gaze back to him as he commented, "That satisfied smirk on your face says you believe she could like you. It also says you believe she will overlook Prophet's outer beauty to see your inner beauty."

"Inner beauty?" Thanatos snorted, confused by the man's words. He'd never heard of someone having inner beauty before.

"Yeah, I heard you and Mad Dog a few days ago," the mortal mentioned. "You were telling him how women tend to cower away from you because of your size and 'permanent frown,' I believe you called it. I think that when the right lady comes along, she'll not be so worried about the outer appearance, but dig deep to see who you are on the inside." The man laughed, turning his head slightly away as his face turned red, showing his embarrassment. "Sorry, my sister is a psychiatrist, and I tend to know almost as much as she does because I've been studying her schoolbooks. I don't want to be a mechanic for the rest of my life, and psychiatry interests me."

Interested in what else the man might tell him, he admitted, "Well, she did smile at me, and she didn't whimper in fear or shudder like a lot of women do when they see me coming. I liked that about her."

"Well, I will admit you do tend to make most of us here nervous," the mortal mentioned. "It's more of a chill we get when you're around, which raises the hair on the arms. It's a downright odd feeling if I'm honest, but I try and ignore it because you've given me no reason to fear you."

Thanatos nodded, knowing the reason for the chill the mortal mentioned was because he was death personified. "I took it as a good sign how she reacted well to me. However, her brother didn't think much of me when I met him later. He was, in fact, quite angry. As soon as Andrina introduced me to him, he began throwing insults my way."

The mortal laughed and explained, "Oh, well, that's normal. Most brothers don't think any guy is good enough for their sister. My sister has been married for two years, and I still think her husband is a douchebag because he got drunk at her birthday party the year they were dating and made my sister cry. I gave him a black eye, and my brother broke his nose before we told him he better never be the cause of her tears again. We made it clear that if he were, nobody would ever find his body."

"He must have had some redeeming qualities; after all, she did marry him," Thanatos reminded the mortal.

The mortal sighed, and with a shrug, he replied, "Yeah. He makes her smile, the kind of smile that lights up her whole face, and he stares at her as if she is his very reason to live."

"Mad Dog and Doom gaze at their ol' ladies like

that. Now that I think about it, the women return those adoring expressions whether the men are paying attention or not, ," Thanatos mentioned thoughtfully.

The mortal nodded before picking up the wrench he'd laid on the front of the car. Sitting back down on the floor, he prepared to slide back under the vehicle once more. Pausing and pointing his wrench at himself to emphasize, he mentioned, "When I find my ol' lady, I want people to say that I look at her that way too. I figure if others can see it, then I must be doing something right."

"Yeah," Thanatos murmured as he turned to walked away and let the man do his job. He paused, glancing over his shoulder to ask, "By the way, what's your name?"

"Name's Jim," the mortal replied before he slid back under the vehicle.

"Nice talking with you Jim, you've given me a lot to think about," Thanatos informed him before turning and striding away.

Two days later, Thanatos found himself standing in the open door of the garage, his shoulder propped against the door jamb, one hand in his pocket, the other holding a sandwich he was slowly eating. He was watching one of the mortals Zeus had hired change a tire while talking to the owner of the car and killing time.

The garage had been getting more and more business lately it seemed. Although, Thanatos had to wonder if a lot of it stemmed more from the mortal's curiosity over the MC than by how good their mechanics were. Not that it mattered one way or the other to him. So long as Zeus allowed them to hire mortals to do the work, he couldn't care less about how the business came to be. He and Apollo mostly just walked around the mechanic side of the shop and pretended to work. They didn't do anything on the auto-body side because it was run entirely by the mortals.

He was staying out of Zeus' sight as of right now as he tried to decide what the best way to see Andrina again was. It had been three days, and he was going crazy with the need to see her. He was seriously thinking about using his godly skills to find her since he didn't have a phone number where he could reach her. Or he could show up at her house and face the wrath of her brother.

He snorted to keep from bursting into laughter at the idea of the boy stopping him. *That punk can't stop me if I wish to see her. I suppose, though, I'll have to at least attempt to get along with him if I want to make Andrina my own; after all, he is her brother.*

"Skull stop staring at the workers and do some work of your own," Zeus yelled from somewhere behind him.

Thanatos was pulled from his thoughts as he swallowed the last bite of his sandwich. Turning, he glared at the bossy Greek god, who only laughed before turning and walking away. He shook his head; Zeus had been acting odd ever since one of the *Moirai* had shown up at Ares' wedding and told him he needed to change his ways. He was still as irritating as a gnat flying about the ear and bossy, but he was also different in a way Thanatos couldn't quite put his finger on.

"Man, do you see that? It isn't often you see a limo on this side of town," one of the mortals excitedly said as he headed out the door.

Thanatos frowned as he watched the vehicle roll slowly into the lot. *Who would be coming here in a limo? If you can afford a limo, you have enough money to take it to a dealership instead of a place like this.*

The driver exited the limo and opened the back door. A woman with long dark brown hair, her back to Thanatos, stepped from the vehicle. "Thank you, Gerald. You may go now, and I'll call if I need you."

The woman's voice is so familiar. It can't be who I think

it is, could it? Thanatos tensely stood, waiting for her to turn.

"Yes, Miss," Gerald replied with a slight bow. He then closed the door, got back in the car, and drove off.

The woman turned, and Thanatos felt his body relax, his heart pounding. *Andrina.* She glanced around as if she were searching for someone, *hopefully for me.* Not wanting to take any chances of the other workers getting to her first, Thanatos headed her way in swift strides.

Andrina grinned when she spotted him and shouted, "Crusher!"

Reaching her, Thanatos leaned in, kissed her cheek, and murmured, "I have missed you. I planned to find a way to see you today, but it would seem you had the same idea."

Andrina laughed and wrapped her arms around his waist as she told him, "I did, and decided to come here when I realized you had no way to get ahold of me. Besides, since my brother has been watching me like a hawk, I thought it would be best if you didn't show up at my front door."

"Mm—I suppose not, but your brother will not stop me if I decide to visit you," Thanatos warned her with a dark look.

"He threatened to lock me in my room," Andrina

told him in a matter-a-fact way. "Instead, he ended up taking my car keys. I had to resort to calling Gerald and taking the limo. Mom is usually the only one who uses it unless we're all going together to a social function."

"Well, I'm glad you came to see me," Thanatos told her. Then, even though he'd already eaten, he asked, "How about we go get some lunch?"

Andrina grinned, and after squeezing his waist, she stepped back. He already missed the feel of her lush body against his.

"I'd like that," she agreed. "I wore jeans, just in case you wanted to take your motorcycle."

Thanatos was the one to grin this time. Just the thought of her pressed up against his back had his heart pounding and his body waking up. It had been a long time since he'd been with a woman, and this one had him straining behind his zipper. Wrapping his arm around her neck, he began to guide her toward his motorcycle. "Let's go."

Once they were both astride, he headed away from the garage and into the heart of town. There was a little diner, Marlo's, they all liked to go to, and it was the first place they'd gone when they'd come to town. Most everyone there was used to them coming in randomly, sometimes in large groups and sometimes only one or two at a time.

Upon arriving, Thanatos helped her off his motor-cycle, then kept holding her hand as he led her to the door of Marlo's Diner. After he'd opened the door, he nudged her to go in ahead of him.

Stepping inside, Andrina gazed around, smiling slightly. She told him, "I've never been here before, but the food smells good."

With his arm once more around her neck, he led her toward a back-corner booth as he said, "The MC comes here quite often. The truth is, this is where Doom met his ol' lady, Irina."

"I think I'd like to meet her," Andrina murmured.

"You'll like her, she's a nice woman, and I'm sure you will meet her," Thanatos murmured back as they were seated.

"Hello, my name is Jenny, and I'll be your server today. What may I get you to drink?" a waitress asked as she came to stand beside the table.

"I'll just have water," Andrina said.

"Same," Thanatos murmured low.

Jenny nodded at them before walking away.

Thanatos sighed because he'd felt the woman's nervousness at being around him. He understood that the mortals couldn't help the nervous feelings they had because of the chills he gave them; it was what it was. Still, he hated it and was so ready to leave the mortal realm behind. Glancing across the tabletop at

Andrina, he allowed himself to watch her as she stared at her menu. *Yet, there sits one excellent reason to stay in this realm for a little longer. Perhaps she would be willing to leave with me when I go.* He shook his head slightly. *No, best not to get ahead of myself. She's only just met me, and even though my feelings for her are already strong, it might take her longer to get there.*

Not bothering to pick up his menu since he already knew what he wanted, he asked, "So, what would you like to eat?"

Andrina bit her lip and said, "I should have the salad, but the Philly steak here is delicious ."

"Then get it," he encouraged her.

"I shouldn't because I need to lose a bit of weight," Andrina informed him. "I've gained enough that my clothes are becoming too tight." Her cheeks then turned pink as she put her hand over her mouth, staring at him. "I'm sorry. You didn't need to know that about me. Sometimes my mouth has no filter."

Thanatos shook his head at her and said, "Andrina, I think you are perfect the way you are. You have a luscious womanly body that makes a man dream of making it his and his alone."

Andrina's cheeks were now flame red, and she dropped her eyes to the table at his words.

Just then, the waitress returned for their order, and Thanatos looked up at her. When Andrina said nothing, he decided to order for them both, saying, "I'll take the house club with fries, and the lady will have the Philly steak with fries."

The waitress quickly wrote down their orders, collected the menus, and left.

CHAPTER FOUR

Thanatos turned his attention back to the beautiful woman across from him. She didn't know it yet, but she would soon be his. She was a temptation that pulled on every piece of him, including his heart, and he wasn't going to let her go. One way or another, he would be making her his.

"I really should eat the salad," she glumly muttered as she stared at the tabletop.

He chuckled and moved over to sit next to her. His move caused her head to come up, and her eyes widened as she watched him.

"Mm—you are a delectable morsel, Andrina, and I like you just the way you are. Why do girls think they need to be a stick-thin, hm?" Thanatos asked, yet he didn't expect an answer. Instead, he then answered the question himself by saying, "Andrina, someone might have told you that thin is better, but it isn't always so. There is such a thing as being too thin, and when you reach that stage, you look weak and sickly. I don't want that for you. I want you to be healthy in mind and body."

"Oh, well, I suppose I'm not fat…"

"No, you are not. We Greek men love curves on our woman and make no mistake; you will be my woman. Andrina, are a curvy temptation that I wish to taste with my lips and my hands," Thanatos murmured close to her ear. He then took a nip at it before he continued, "I am a big man with big hands. Those beautiful breasts of yours would fill them perfectly, and if we weren't in public right now, I would prove that to you. Don't get me started on those hips of yours. Those hips of yours would fill my imagination with ideas of how I would hold you as I loved you into oblivion."

Andrina moaned, her eyes slightly closed as she leaned into him.

His hand moved over her thigh, lightly squeezing as he continued, "The feel of your thighs squeezing me as you sat behind me on my motorcycle had me biting back my need to have you under me in a bed. Even now, I can almost feel your thighs gripping my hips as

I make love to you, giving you all the pleasure you can take and more."

"Crusher, you shouldn't talk so blatantly about those things. We aren't married, and someone might hear you," Andrina whispered, her face red with embarrassment. Yet her voice was filled with longing as if she needed to hear that she was desirable.

"Maybe I shouldn't, but you know you want it," he whispered gently. "You know you want me as much as I want you, and if it is a marriage you want, I will give you that too. Just know that the *Moirai* have brought us together for a reason, and I will never deny the gift they have given me. You are a gift, Andrina, a gift for a man who has been alone too long."

"The *Moirai*, the fates." Andrina's eyes opened to gaze into his, searching. A smile lit her face as she seemed to find what she was looking for, and she whispered, "I'm a gift?"

"A gift," he agreed. "I will make you mine soon, twining our life threads together in the tapestry of life should the *Moirai* will it, and I believe they have. I will not allow you to slip away from me," he straightened up, pulling away from her, "but first we will have lunch and get to know each other better."

"Okay," she agreed as he moved back to his side of the table, and the waitress returned with their food.

Thanatos wanted to sit next to her, but if he didn't move, he feared he would ravish her right there because his body and soul wanted her. He needed that little bit of space to cool off.

They began to eat in silence, but after a moment, Andrina asked, "So, do you have any siblings?"

"I do. I even have a twin brother."

Her eyes widened, and she lay her sandwich down, saying, "There are two of you? Is he as big as you are?" She paused, then thumped herself lightly on the forehead before answering her question. "Of course, he is. The two of you are twins, making the question a dumb one for me to be asking."

The words left her mouth innocently enough, but as soon as they were out, she saw the hurt cross his features. Then his face went blank, and he looked away.

Andrina realized then how much his height seemed to bother him, just as her wide hips bothered her. She didn't know why exactly and honestly didn't need to. All she knew was he had made her feel good about herself, despite her thick waistline. She didn't like thinking she had hurt him and wanted to make him feel better about his height too.

Getting up, she slid in next to him and hugged him around the waist tightly as she said, "Crusher, I'm sorry. I didn't mean to make you feel bad. I think you are perfect in your way; I've just never known anyone as tall and broad as you are before. I went to school with a guy who was about six feet four inches with a slim build, and he played basketball with my brother. His name was Jerome, and he was a sweet but shy guy. I think perhaps you're even taller than he was though."

"I am. I'm just over seven feet," Thanatos agreed as he wrapped an arm around her. Humming softly with content, he placed his chin lightly on top of her head. "I scare women, Andrina, always have. Most can barely stand to be within a few feet of me once they see how tall I am. I've also heard from multiple sources how the expression on my face isn't exactly pleasant to look upon either."

Andrina laughed as she moved her head back so she could gaze up into his face. Her eyes roamed over his face, taking in the slant of his thick dark eyebrows over his eyes, and perhaps it did make him look as if he were mad, but it didn't bother her. "I went home and told my mom you were charming and had Greek god-like looks. I don't find your height intimidating, and I don't see anything about your face that would cause me to turn away from you. I like you, Crusher, a lot, and the more time I spend with you, the more time I want to spend with you. So, if you can live with my few extra pounds, I can live with your few extra inches in height. Crusher, I know you think you are built like a Mack truck, but it honestly doesn't bother me."

"Built like a Mack truck? I'm guessing that means I'm broad across the chest and muscular everywhere else?" Thanatos chuckled when she nodded, and he kissed her cheek before saying, "I believe those two things will be in perfect harmony when I make love to you, *glyké mou peirasmé*."

Andrina felt like squealing in happiness even as she felt her cheeks heat at his words. *He called me "my sweet temptation" again.* Excited as it made her, she still felt the need to clarify things. So, clearing her throat, she asked, "Aren't you moving a bit fast here?"

Thanatos shook his head at her and declared, "*Óchi*, I am not. Haven't you ever heard of love at first sight? I fell for you the moment I gazed into those big green eyes of yours, and I have no intention of ever letting you go."

Andrina almost swooned at his sweet words, but what he'd said also made her believe her feelings might not all be one-sided. For she was beginning to feel a draw toward him too, and the thought of Thanatos ever leaving made her heart feel heavy. Still, because her thoughts were chaotic, she wasn't sure what to say. So, she just gave him a nod and pulled her plate across the table, having decided she didn't want to sit apart from him, not even to eat.

Thanatos took a deep breath, willing his body to calm down. He watched as Andrina picked up her sandwich and resumed her eating. Following her lead, he did the same, and for a few moments, they ate in silence. Finally, he asked, "Tell me, what do you do? Are you in school, or do you work somewhere?"

"Oh, well, you see…" Andrina began, only to stop and sigh as she dragged her French fry around in ketchup. "Okay, first I should tell you how I just found out that some of our money came from our father in his will. We didn't know this until the day you dropped me at home."

"Okay," he murmured. "So, your father was well off, and he left money for your mom?"

"He did," Andrina agreed as she lay the French fry down and peered up at him. "Apparently, when Mom received the money, she invested most of it and invested it well. Mom kept out just enough to support us while she went back to school and to pay for her schooling to get a degree in psychology. Once Mom had her degree, she took just a small amount of the money she'd made with investments and used it to hire someone to take care of us until her career took off. Once that happened, Mom took some of the money she had left, and divided it between Kristos and me.

"It seems that by that time, Mom had made a good friend who helped her invest the money even better, and soon the original sum had tripled. By the time Kristos and I were sixteen, the amount had grown by a *lot*. So, she gave each of us a percentage of it to invest on our own, leaving each of us with more than enough to call ourselves wealthy. However, we can't touch it until we're twenty-five in two years."

"So, you and your brother are well off in your own right," he commented. "This would explain his attitude the other day."

Andrina laughed before saying, "Yeah, he does tend to think highly of himself. Investing in stocks interested him, though, so Kristos became an investment banker and is doing very well for himself."

"What about you?"

"Ah, well," Andrina said as she flushed and stared at her plate. "I'm struggling a bit more and living more on the interest of my investment money than on any money I've earned. You see, I'm an artist at heart, and sadly it can be hard to make your way in the art world."

"What kind of art exactly?"

"I started with painting before moving on to sculpting," Andrina told him. "I work part-time at that little boutique I was coming out of when I ran into you. It gives me a little job experience, a little spending money, and it leaves me plenty of time to work on my sculptures. Plus, they sometimes allow me to sell my artworks there."

"Have you sold anything?"

"I have, but just a few pieces," she said. "It hasn't been nearly enough to get my name out there, but better than nothing, I suppose. Mom keeps telling me I'm young, I have plenty of time, but I get impatient sometimes."

"You said you'd get you money in two years. That would make you twenty-three."

"Yeah, and to hear my mom tell it, I still have my best years ahead of me."

The rest of the meal went by quickly as they talked about mundane things. When they'd finished, Thanatos paid the bill, and they walked out the door and into the bright sunshine. Once outside, they followed the sidewalk to where he'd parked his motorcycle.

"Is there somewhere special you'd like me to drop you off at?"

Andrina sighed as she stared straight ahead. She

then glanced up at him from under her lashes as she said, "I suppose you could take me home."

Thanatos stopped walking and turned to face her. Cocking his head as he placed a forefinger under her chin, he tilted her head up. Once he was gazing directly into her eyes, he stated, "You don't sound very sure about that at all."

"Well, it is a workday for you, so I figured you probably needed to head back to work. I didn't want to keep you if you needed to go."

"I don't," Thanatos informed her. *My job is basically nothing but a ruse. Will anyone genuinely care if I'm there?* Making a quick decision, he added, "I think I'd like to spend more time with you instead, so I believe I'll take you home with me. Do you need to let anyone know you won't be home anytime soon?"

Andrina shook her head and softly answered, "No, I'm old enough. I don't answer to my mom anymore about my coming and going. If Kristos wants to be a pain in my derriere and raise a fuss, I'll remind him that he's my brother, not my father."

"Good, you are mine for the day then," he advised her as he handed her a helmet.

"I have no problem with that, at all."

Thanatos grinned at her before mounting his motorcycle. He then held out a hand and helped her climb on behind him. Once she was safely on, he started it up and took off for his home.

Thanatos pulled his motorcycle up into his garage, rolling to a stop and shutting off the engine as he closed the garage door behind him. Helping Andrina off, he took the helmet she offered him after she'd taken it off. Placing it on the shelf along the wall, he grabbed her hand as he said, "Come along, let's go inside."

They entered the kitchen from the garage, and he led her into his living room where they took a seat on his couch.

"This is a really beautiful house from what little I've seen," Andrina said as she surveyed the room.

Glancing around, he tried to see it from her perspective. Thanatos had decorated the living room in earth tones, browns, beige, and cream. He had a dark brown leather and recliner, a cream-colored area rug covering most of the hardwood floor, and beige and brown striped drapes. Except for the coffee table and two end tables which held lamps, that was all his furnishings. He wondered if she thought it too spartan because, for him, it was just a place to crash when he needed somewhere to sleep. Of course, as a god, he didn't need much sleep. Which meant he spent truly little time here, and everything she saw was almost new. "Thank you."

"How many rooms do you have. I noticed when we were driving up that it looked quite large," Andrina commented.

"There are three bedrooms and one bathroom upstairs, all but one bedroom unfurnished and unused. Downstairs is the kitchen, dining room, laundry room, the master bedroom and bath, a guest half-bath, family room, and living room. I also have a basement that I use as a game and weight room."

"That seems a bit big for one person," Andrina murmured with a raised eyebrow.

"It is, but sometimes my brother comes and stays with me," Thanatos explained. "I'm not here much, though. I spend most of my time at the clubhouse or the garage."

"Mm-hm… so, why such a big house?"

Thanatos shrugged and answered, "I saw it, liked it, and decided to get it. I have plenty of money, and it will be a good investment if I ever decide to sell it."

Of course, Thanatos wasn't exactly telling her the truth, that he was only here temporarily. He had bought this home because he genuinely did like it. It was so light and airy, much different from his home in the Underworld. He also knew it was a home that a family would enjoy. After Hades and Ares had married, it had given Thanatos hope that maybe he might be able to find a woman that would feel for him the way Irina felt for Hades and how Cathy felt for Ares. He knew that if he did, as a mortal, she would want to be here some of the time at least, especially if she had family that would like to visit.

Now that he had found Andrina, that hope was coming true for him, and she did have family that might visit. Although they lived in the same town, meaning overnight visits wouldn't happen. However, sometimes his brother did come and stay with him.

"So, if I'm honest," Andrina began as she turned slightly to look at him. "I can't truly picture you as a mechanic."

Thanatos chuckled and sat back. Feeling the urge to make himself comfortable, he propped his feet on the coffee table in front of him and crossed his arms as he gazed at her, lost in her beauty. "Me either. When Tank dragged us all into this, I think we all felt that way."

"Dragged you into opening a mechanic garage and an auto-body shop?"

Thanatos took in a sharp breath as he looked away from her. He'd almost given her information he should be keeping to himself because he felt so comfortable with her. *At least I didn't say, Zeus. How quick can I tell her the truth of it all anyway? I want her to know the real me, good and bad. I don't have to hide who I truly am from her.*

"Um—Crusher?"

Thanatos turned to look at her, knowing, at least for now, he would have to settle for half-truths. So, giving a heavy sigh, he said, "Sorry. The truth is, I never wanted to be in a motorcycle club, but Tank tends to drag us all into doing things we don't honestly want to do."

"Us?" Andrina questioned with a quirk of her brow.

"Me and a lot of our friends," Thanatos murmured.

"You've known him a long time then?"

"I have," Thanatos agreed. "Tank tends to talk us into doing things even when we aren't sure it's the best thing to be doing."

"I had a friend like that one time. She drove me nuts because she was always pulling me into one of her schemes," Andrina mentioned, giving his thigh a pat to show she understood.. "I finally grew tired of constantly being in trouble at school because of her and cut ties with her. I see her in town sometimes, and when possible, I turn and go the other way to avoid her."

"Does she still try to cause you problems?"

Andrina huffed out a slight laugh before saying,

"No, but only because I'm able to avoid her most of the time. Seriously though, if I were to confront her, she would probably rip my hair out after starting a catfight. We didn't exactly part on the best of terms."

"Sounds as if the best thing to do is avoid her then."

"My thoughts exactly. What I'm trying to say though, is that I understand what it's like," Andrina told him.

CHAPTER FIVE

Thanatos gave Andrina a slight nod of understanding at her words. Sometimes the easiest way to prevent conflict is to avoid the one who tended to start it.

"So, if you didn't want to be a mechanic, why do it?" Andrina asked him.

Thanatos shrugged and answered, "I don't do much; I just pretend I am while someone else does the bulk of the work."

Andrina laughed out loud as she lay her head on the back of the couch facing him. When her laughter finally subsided, she wiped the tears from her eyes and said, "It sounds to me as if, in your own way, you're rebelling against Tank. Does he realize what you're doing?"

Thanatos once more shrugged and said, "Who

cares if he does or not. I'm not a mechanic and never will be. I'm much too pretty to be a grease monkey, don't you agree?"

That started her laughing again, and Thanatos had to grin. He loved to hear her laughter, and he loved that he could make her laugh instead of run. He sighed as he observed her pink cheeks and her wide smile. Both were so beautiful. The joy on her face made her even more of a temptation than usual, and it caused him to want to kiss her desperately.

Leaning toward her, his eyes locked on hers, he listened as her laugher stopped, but joy remained on her face. He heard her breath hitch as he stared into her eyes. When he leaned even closer, she leaned in also, and their lips touched. He was barely able to contain a groan at the feel of those plump and moist lips. As if it had a mind of its own, his hand rose up to tangle in her hair, tilting her head to kiss her deeper, nipping her lower lip until she opened to him.

Andrina moaned as her own hands came up to wrap around his neck.

Eventually, Thanatos pulled back, and they both took a much-needed breath. He softly admitted, "I don't know if I should have done that, but the temptation of you was suddenly just too much for me."

Andrina smiled as she told him, "I have been

hoping for a kiss from you. I wanted to know what your lips would feel like against mine."

Thanatos leaned back in, his lips almost touching hers, as he asked, "So, may I have another?"

She nodded.

Thanatos pulled her onto his lap so that they were in a less awkward position as their lips met once more. When the kiss was over, she lay her head on his shoulder, and he hummed with contentment. She felt so good in his arms, he never wanted to let her go.

A phone began ringing, and Andrina jerked, startled, causing him to tighten his arms around her.

"Sorry, that's mine," she murmured. Thanatos let her go, and she got up, grabbing her purse where she'd placed it on the floor at the end of the couch. Pulling her cellphone out of a side pocket as she returned to her seat, she answered, "Hello?"

Thanatos watched as the smile left her face, and an irritated look replaced it.

"You aren't my boss, Kristos, so it doesn't matter where I am. I'm a grown woman and can come and go as I please…" Andrina said. After a moment of silence on her end, she continued, "Oh, and I didn't appreciate you hiding my car keys either, yet you did it."

There was a long silence, during which Andrina seemed to be grinding her teeth. Thanatos wondered if Kristos was giving her a lecture.

"Kristos, Mom knew I was leaving and even where I planned to go, so it isn't like I disappeared completely." She paused, frowning at the floor as she listened. Then, sounding completely exasperated, she exclaimed, "Oh, get a life, Kristos, and let me live mine!" She hung up and growled as she stared at her phone. "Sometimes..."

Thanatos pulled her back onto his lap and kissed her again.

"Mm, that's one way to take away a person's bad mood," Andrina mentioned when their lips parted from another kiss.

"I agree," he said, "and yours are so addictive."

"I suppose you realized that that was my brother?"

"The name Kristos kind of gave that away," he agreed as he threaded his fingers through her hair.

Andrina heaved a heavy sigh as she laid her head on his shoulder before saying, "Kristos wants to be my boss, and when we were kids, I tended to let him because I was shy and self-conscious. It was easier just to let him take the lead, and he kept the bullies away."

"Bullies?" Thanatos questioned. Anger rose in him at the idea of anyone bullying this sweet woman, and his body tensed as his hand clenched into a fist full of her hair.

Andrina tilted her head, now staring him square in

the eyes as she replied, "Yes, bullies. We had enough money for both of us to be accepted by the high class, and Kristos was. However, I was fat enough that I was not. I'm not as big as I was then; puberty helped, but I'm still not truly accepted by most of the ones Kristos calls his friends. Too many stick-thin girls and buff boys," she said with a sigh. "They smile to my face when he's around but make snide comments when he isn't."

Thanatos felt like snarling, wondering how her brother could let it happen. Needing to know why, he asked, "Does your brother know this goes on?"

Andrina shrugged, leaning back into him as she answered, "I don't say too much about it. I mostly just try and be gone if I know they're coming over. Crusher, I love my brother. Yes, sometimes he annoys me and gives me headaches, but I still love him. I don't want to make him feel he can't have his friends because of me."

"It isn't right that they treat you that way though," Thanatos angrily grunted. "Andrina, if your brother cares about you, he wouldn't want to be friends with those who make your life miserable."

Andrina let out a heavy sigh before she whispered, "I know, but…"

"Sweetheart, you should tell him, be honest with

him," Thanatos murmured. He felt his gut tighten as he thought about the half-truths, he was feeding her about himself. It made him feel like a hypocrite, and he didn't like it, which caused him to murmur, "Andrina, I need to..."

A banging on his front door had his head coming up as Thanatos stopped talking. Frowning as he glanced over, he wondered who would be at his door. So, after gently placing Andrina on the couch, he stood and began to head toward the door.

"Were you expecting someone?" Andrina asked him as she stood also.

"*Óchi*, I rarely have company," Thanatos told her, although he had an idea who it might be.

Opening the door, Thanatos ended up with a fist to the face.

"Where is my sister, you freak?" Kristos yelled, fist still balled up as if to hit Thanatos again if he didn't like his answer.

Thanatos moved his hand up to his nose, which was now gushing blood everywhere, his eyebrows raised at the gall of the young mortal. It had been a long time since someone had dared to hit him, and that had been his brother. The hit hadn't hurt, but it connected in just the right spot to cause a nosebleed, probably making it seem a whole lot worse than it actually was.

Regardless, the idea of this mortal thinking he could hit the Greek god of death had Thanatos growling in anger. Stepping out onto the porch, he reached out to grab Kristos by the collar. He was lifting Kristos off his feet just as Andrina stepped into the doorway behind him.

"Kristos?" Andrina questioned in a shocked voice.

"Who do you think you are coming to my home and assaulting me?" Thanatos asked Kristos.

"I don't want my sister anywhere near you!" Kristos shouted. He struggled to loosen Thanatos' hold on him, yanking at his hand.

"Kristos! You—" Andrina's voice trailed off as she moved around Thanatos to step out onto the porch with them. "Crusher, your nose is bleeding, and there's blood everywhere. Kristos, did you hit him? Why would you do that?"

"He deserves to be hit, and more, for messing with you, Andrina!" Kristos yelled as he turned his head slightly to peek at Andrina. "I told him to stay away from you, and I meant it."

"Put him down, Crusher, please," Andrina pleaded as she tugged at Thanatos' arm. "How did you even find me, Kristos?"

Thanatos put her brother down and began to step back. This fight was now between Andrina and her brother, and he would respect that.

"Mom told me you'd gone off to see your 'biker friend' when I asked why you weren't having lunch with us. So, I tracked the GPS on your phone after calling you," Kristos explained as he reached out to try and grab ahold of her arm. "Now, you're coming home with me because you shouldn't be here. So, let's go."

Andrina stepped back, avoiding her brother's reach, and moved slightly behind Thanatos.

Thanatos took her move to mean she wasn't willing to go with her brother and quickly moved between Kristos and Andrina. She wasn't going anywhere if she didn't want to, and he didn't want her to leave anyway. "Don't touch her. I will take her home when she is ready to leave."

"She's my sister, and if I say she's leaving, then she's leaving," Kristos argued as he tried to reach around Thanatos and grab Andrina.

Thanatos snatched his arm before Kristos could reach her and twisted it slightly.

The move caused Kristos to yelp in pain before yelling, "Let me go, you freakish brute!"

"I will let you go when you leave your sister be," Thanatos said coldly. "She is a grown woman, not a child to be drug home by her brother. She is perfectly capable of making her own decisions, and it seems to me your mother knows that since she seemingly had no issue with Andrina coming to see me, even if you do not."

"Is there a problem here, brother?" a deep voice called out and asked from the far corner of the house.

Thanatos didn't even have to turn to know the voice was that of his brother Hypnos. He didn't know precisely when his brother had shown up, but all the same, he replied, "I've got it under control, Hypnos, but thank you."

"*Nai*, it appears as if you have it under control. You do know you have blood dripping off your chin right now, don't you?" Hypnos sarcastically mentioned as he stepped out of the shadows and into the sunlight.

"*Nai*, brother, I do know because I can feel it. However, thanks for stating the obvious," Thanatos answered back just as sarcastic.

"That's what brothers are for," Hypnos snickered.

"There are two of you freaks?" Kristos asked with a shout. It seemed as if he was about to pop a blood vessel at any moment as he turned his head back and forth between the two brothers.

"Kristos, manners! What would Mom say if she could hear you right now?" Andrina scolded as she moved forward to slap her brother on the shoulder.

Thanatos watched from the corner of his eye as Andrina turned from glaring at her brother to face his brother.

Hypnos was now standing just off to the side of the porch. He had a sardonic grin on his face as he watched the drama.

"Hello. It's so nice to meet you. I'm Andrina, and the fool being stupid is my brother Kristos," Andrina said politely.

"Hello, Andrina, it is nice to meet you also," Hypnos said as he gave her a slight bow of his head. "My name is Hypnos."

Andrina laughed as she said, "So, does Crusher crush their skulls before or after you put them to sleep?"

Hypnos shot Thanatos a slightly confused look before chuckling. Then he murmured, "Either way is fine with us, but I suppose it depends on who gets there first."

Hypnos hadn't been dragged into the MC roleplay as Thanatos had been. He'd been away working when Zeus had come calling on Hades that day, so he hadn't been with Thanatos, or he might have ended up coming also. With a name like Hypnos though, it was apparent that Andrina thought he was part of the MC, which was fine because it meant she wouldn't question his odd name. Thankfully, Andrina hadn't noticed the slight confusion Hypnos had shown at her question before his face had cleared, which could have had her asking questions.

"This is nice, a reunion of freaks and all, but give me my sister, and I'll be on my way," Kristos smarted off, seemingly tired of listening to the chit-chat. He was staring mulishly at Thanatos, his arms crossed, trying his best to intimidate the larger man.

Thanatos snorted at the intimidation antics; they weren't working because the boy was a runt compared to him. Slim build and minimal muscle tone. So, just to be annoying, Thanatos flexed his biceps before crossing his arms over his chest. He chuckled softly as Kristos's eyes widened.

Through gritted teeth, Andrina muttered, "Kristos," anger evident in her tone.

Thanatos gave a huge sigh, dropping his arms to his side as he grunted in irritation at the whole fiasco. All he'd wanted was to spend the afternoon with the sweet temptation known as Andrina, not cause chaos with her brother that she would have to go home to later. "Hypnos, I believe I'll accept your offer of help after all."

Hypnos raised an eyebrow, unsure where this was all going. He didn't know the girl or the boy either, for that matter, and had no idea why either of them was here. Both were mortal, and his brother rarely spent time with mortals, so why this girl? He'd come up just about the time the boy had begun banging on the door and had stayed out of sight, more curious than anything. It had shocked him when a girl had exited the house. Shaking his head in confusion, he wasn't sure his brother knew what he was doing befriending a mortal, so he questioned, "The girl?"

Thanatos and Hypnos both turned their attention to Andrina. She was standing, arms crossed, foot-tapping, and glaring at her brother as if she wanted to strangle him.

"I was going to explain things to her anyway," Thanatos softly answered.

"Ah…" Hypnos murmured as things suddenly clicked into place. He'd heard two of the gods had fallen in love. "You have succumbed to the draw of a woman just as the other two have."

Thanatos nodded and agreed, "I have."

"I will help you then," Hypnos said because he wished his brother to have happiness.

Hypnos and Thanatos were remarkably close. He knew being the god of death was hard on Thanatos because most everyone felt the chill of death around him and steered clear. With mortals being so uncomfortable in his presence, he'd had very few friends during his life span and even fewer lovers.

Hypnos let out a silent sigh before he waved his

hand toward Kristos. When he did, the boy slumped, his eyes closing in sleep. Hypnos quickly stepped forward and grabbed Kristos as he fell backward toward the edge of the porch before he could hit the ground.

Andrina cried out, reaching out toward her brother's now sleeping body as she asked, "What happened to him?"

"He is not harmed," Thanatos informed her as he held her back, "he is only asleep. My brother's name is Hypnos for a reason."

"But…" Andrina's eyes were wide and full of confusion as she glanced over at Hypnos.

Hypnos only shrugged. It wasn't his responsibility to give the mortal the answers she was seeking. "Do not turn to me for the answers you seek."

Andrina turned her eyes back to Thanatos.

"I will explain, I promise," Thanatos told her.

"What do I do with him?" Hypnos asked as he put the boy over his shoulder.

"Take him home, put him to bed, and I'll deal with the backlash of it all later," Thanatos said before giving Hypnos the address.

Hypnos gave his brother a slight nod even as he said, "It was nice to meet you, Andrina. Until next time, goodbye."

"Goodbye."

"Later, my brother," Thanatos added.

Hypnos walked toward the corner of the house, and once he had reached the shadows, he left in a cloud of gray smoke to take the mortal back to his home.

Thanatos quickly drew Andrina inside as Hypnos disappeared around the side of the house. He didn't want to take any chances of Andrina seeing Hypnos disappear with her brother. He needed to explain who they were before she saw any of their godly powers.

"Crusher, what's going on?" Andrina asked. "Why did my brother suddenly go to sleep like that?"

Thanatos led her to the sofa, and after they had sat, he took both of her hands in his. Gazing into her beautiful eyes, he began, "Before your brother came banging on my door, I was about to explain a few things to you about myself. Do you mind if I start with that? It will explain a lot, I promise."

Andrina took a deep breath and opened her mouth as if to say something, only to close it again. Finally, with a nod of agreement, she whispered, "Okay."

Thanatos took a deep breath, letting it out slowly as he collected his thoughts. He decided to begin with, "I know everything I'm about to tell you will most likely seem far-fetched and ridiculous, but it will all be true. I want to start by telling you, though, that I have lived a long time and have met many women, yet none have intrigued me as much as you do. I found myself falling in love with you from the moment I met you on the sidewalk that day."

CHAPTER SIX

"Isn't that a bit fast?" Andrina whispered, her green eyes wide as they gazed into his dark ones.

She would be the first to admit that she didn't know a lot about MCs, but she'd heard they could be a rough crowd. So, she figured he wasn't exactly an angel, but she'd quickly realized she didn't care because she genuinely liked him and his kisses.

This love at first sight thing though, is something I've only read about in books. Indeed, there can't be any truth to it. Either way, I'll listen with an open mind to what he wishes to tell me.

Letting go of one of her hands, he reached up to caress her cheek as he murmured, "No, at least it wasn't for me. I have lived long enough to see the difference between fake love and true love. I once had feelings for a woman, and she bore me a daughter,

Erin. Thinking back, I know it wasn't real love, and that's probably why the relationship didn't last. Recently, I have watched two men I respect fall in love and have watched how the women they fell in love with have brightened their lives. I realized just by watching them what I have been missing in my life, and suddenly there you were as if the *Moirai* themselves had placed you in my path."

He's talking about the Moirai *now, better known as the fates. He believes the fates placed me in his path.* Andrina was surprised at his words but still willing to listen. So, she cleared her throat before she declared, "I'm listening."

"This is probably going to sound nuts to you, but I promise, no matter how crazy it sounds to you, it is the truth." He sighed, running his hand through his hair. He then lifted his eyes to gaze into hers as he said, "I am Thanatos, the Greek god of death."

Andrina stared at him, barely blinking as she took in his words. She opened her mouth to speak but wasn't sure what to say to his revelation. So, instead, she waited for him to continue.

"As I said, I know it sounds crazy, but hear me out, please. Just give me a chance to tell you everything."

Andrina nodded for him to continue.

Thanatos let out a heavy breath before continuing to explain. "Zeus is easily bored; I suppose we all are after so many centuries of living. Zeus though, when he becomes bored, he tends to drag a bunch of the gods and goddesses into one mad scheme or another."

"Schemes?"

"*Nai*," Thanatos agreed, "except, he calls them games."

"Zeus, king of the Greek gods, *that* Zeus?" Andrina asked next. She was feeling a bit skeptical but still willing to listen to what he had to say.

"*Nai*. Although he is president of the Steel Chariots, MC, he goes by the name Tank, Thanatos revealed. "I don't usually get pulled into these games, but I happened to have a meeting with Hades, and when I showed up for it, Zeus and Poseidon were there. Zeus was telling Hades about the newest game he was planning. He told Hades it was called roleplay, though I'm sure Hades wasn't even listening."

"Interesting," she hummed.

"Of course, Zeus, arrogant god that he is, also planned to put his own twist to it by making it real instead of computerized. It wasn't long before Hades cut him off and told him he didn't want to hear anymore and tried to send them on their way because he had a meeting with me. Knowing Hades as I do, I know he wasn't even listening to most of Zeus's explanation anyway. Nevertheless, Zeus always manages to get the last word in, and he never takes no for an answer. As he's readying to leave, Zeus demanded Hades to be there. He also mentioned how I was welcome to join them. I never dreamed his game would end up lasting as long as it has though."

"So, why did you join in?" Andrina inquired.

Thanatos softly grunted before he explained, "My life isn't exactly fun or even interesting. So, I figured, why not, it might help relieve some of the boredom I face most days, and I spend a lot of time in the mortal realm anyway. Not only that but just because Zeus didn't demand I come, it was mostly an order anyway, since it came from him. Let's face it; if I hadn't shown up, he would have hunted me down at some point."

Andrina blinked a few times, letting everything Thanatos had told her to settle in her mind. Once she had a hold on it, she cleared her throat and asked, "I'm curious, how many of the gods did Zeus rope into coming here?"

"Poseidon, Hades, Ares, Eros, Apollo, Dionysus, and I for the men."

"For the men? Zeus recruited some of the goddesses too, I'm guessing?" Andrina questioned.

"*Nai*, Hera, Aphrodite, Athena, and Artemis," Thanatos answered. "A few of the others show up now and then, just to see what is happening, but those are the main players."

"Huh. So, what exactly do you do in this roleplay?"

"We don't do much, not really. We ride around, sometimes acting tuff and unruly because Zeus being Zeus likes to throw his weight around just to prove he can. We've started a few bar fights and had a few run-ins with the law for disrupting the peace. Nothing significant enough for us to wind up in jail or anything.

"As you know, since you've been there, Zeus has opened the garage, and we now employ roughly eight mortal men, three of whom ended up joining our MC. That means we now must be careful what we do and say so we don't come across as anything but mortal. He pretty much had to hire them because none of us have a clue how to fix a vehicle or how to paint one," Thanatos concluded with a huff. His eyes slightly narrowed as he commented, "You truly are taking this well."

"Oh, well, I'm not sure yet if I believe any of it," Andrina admitted to him. Crossing her arms, she narrowed her eyes at him as she added, "Perhaps everything you've just told me is your game of role-playing, pretending to be a Greek god..."

"I actually can prove I'm Thanatos if you would like me to," Thanatos said softly, wanting—no needing—her to believe him.

Andrina stared at him for long moments, her eyes still narrowed as she reminded him, "You know, my father was Greek. So, I naturally studied the gods and goddesses to learn about his culture. I also studied the Greek language, and I'm fluent in it."

Thanatos nodded, not sure yet where this was going.

Andrina huffed as she stared down at the floor, seemingly deep in thought. Finally, she raised her head, connecting their eyes. "There's not much written about you in the mythology books, so your history is pretty blank. Although, apparently, down through time, you've had many different looks. Some people even believe him to be a demon; you know that, right?"

"I do. I have seen pictures of what mortals consider to be demons, and most, just like me, have black wings and red eyes. If you add in how I live in the Underworld, it would be an easy misconception to make," Thanatos explained.

"You aren't a daemon."

"No, I am not, even if I do have red eyes," Thanatos agreed.

Andrina chuckled.

Thoughtfully, Thanatos continued, "I will admit to having changed my appearance over time as I became bored with it. In the beginning, I was seen as an old man, but later I appeared as a young man in his youth."

"Yes, I believe I read that somewhere," Andrina murmured. "I suppose though, it is only normal for every age to have its ideas about how death himself should look. For most, you have become the Grim Reaper and appear as a skeletal being wearing a black robe and carrying a scythe."

Thanatos wrinkled his nose at that description of himself but murmured his agreement, "*Nai*, that is true, but as you can see, I am not a skeleton. Nor do I turn into one when I retrieve souls," he informed her. "Do you remember what I told you about the decal on my motorcycle?"

Andrina nodded as she replied, "I do. You said it was Thanatos, the Greek god of death. Is that what you look like now?"

"It is, and I have kept that image longer than most because I like it," Thanatos said with a slight smile.

Andrina scooted across the couch cushion, closer to him. She cupped his cheek in her hands as she said, "I like the way you look now too. Could I perhaps see your true form?"

"You now believe I am who I say I am?"

Andrina smiled as she answered, "Well, maybe.

How about I let you prove you are who you say you are."

Thanatos smirked and stood up. Closing his eyes, he took a deep breath and let himself relax. With a slight wave of his hand, he let his mortal façade fade, leaving his true self behind.

Andrina gasped loudly.

Thanatos opened his eyes and found her staring just over his left shoulder. He smiled and flexed his wings, creating a slight breeze that blew her hair slightly back away from her face.

"Your wings are huge," Andrina pronounced as she stood up and moved to stand in front of him.

"They need to be to hold up the weight of a full-grown man."

"May I touch them?"

Thanatos nodded, his heart pounding like a bass drum as he waited for her touch. His wings were ultra-sensitive, and he knew her fingers on them would either please him or cause him anger because that was how touching them worked. Usually, he let no one feel them because of that fact. However, he wanted her to do it because he wanted the pleasurable feelings he was almost positive her stroking his wing would give him.

Andrina reached her hand up and out, only to give a soft huff. Then she stated, "I'm too short. I can't reach the top of them."

Thanatos chuckled before putting his hands around her waist and lifting her. Her hand instantly reached for the top of his wing as her legs wrapped around his waist. A shiver moved through him at her gentle stroking of his feathered appendage, and he felt the stirring of arousal moving through him. He softly groaned, tilting his head forward, only to find this put his forehead in the perfect place to be cushioned by her breasts.

Andrina gasped again, her body stiffening, but her hand stayed on his wing as she asked, "What are you doing?"

Thanatos moved his head back and focused on her as he replied, "The touch of your hand has a powerful effect on me. It has caused almost instant arousal."

"Oh," she whispered. "I didn't mean to…"

"It's okay; you didn't know it would affect me that way," he told her. "Besides, I like the feeling. I don't normally let women close enough to touch my body and rarely let anyone at all touch my wings because they are so sensitive. I think your touch has affected me even stronger than it usually would."

"So, you knew it might affect you in some manner, yet you let me touch them anyway?"

He nodded.

Andrina smiled at him as she carefully leaned down to give him a light kiss on his lips.

Thanatos found that the light kiss wasn't enough; it just created the need for more. So, lowering Andrina slightly, he tilted his head to deepen the kiss, nipping lightly at her lower lip.

Andrina let out a soft moan and opened her mouth, allowing his tongue to invade it. After a moment or two, she broke away, breathless, and murmured, "You make my body feel so hot."

Thanatos chuckled.

Andrina peered at him with her big green eyes and sighed. "Crusher."

"*Nai,* my darling?"

"May I call you Thanatos now?"

"You may, just not in public, of course," he agreed.

"Okay," Andrina agreed. She sighed, leaning her forehead against his as she ran her fingers lightly over his left wing. Whispering, she told him, "It's almost scary how strong my feelings are for you already. Nevertheless, I genuinely believe we need to get to know one another better before we let things get too heated. I'm not the kind of girl who sleeps with a man after just meeting him."

"I know you aren't, and we will slow down even though it is challenging for me to do because you are such a *glykós peirasmós*," he murmured.

"Am I a sweet temptation to you, Thanatos?" she asked, her large green eyes locked in on his.

"*Nai*, you are," Thanatos agreed before giving her a chaste kiss on her lips.

Andrina hummed with a happy smile on her face before laying her head on his shoulder.

Thanatos continued, "If it pleases you, darling, we will move at a slower pace building our relationship because I don't want to rush you into something and have you regret it. Regret me."

"I need to move a bit slower, and I don't want to regret knowing you either," she said.

"Okay, so, how about a few dates?" Thanatos suggested. He tilted his head thoughtfully as he continued to enjoy her hand brushing over his wings. "Not that I know much about dating, so you'll have to help me out."

"I don't know much about dating either," Andrina informed him as she laughed. "I guess it will be the blind leading the blind."

Thanatos chuckled, "Figuring it out together sounds good."

"How about we have what is considered a traditional first date," she suggested. "Dinner and a movie?"

"I think I can handle that," Thanatos murmured as he placed her feet back on the floor. With a wave of his hand, his wings were gone. So, he grabbed her hand tugged her gently back down onto the couch with him.

Andrina sat down next to him and lay her head on his shoulder with a sigh, saying, "Our biggest obstacle to get over is probably going to be my brother. You know that, right?"

"*Óchi*, darling, he won't be a problem because I'll put him in his place if need be," Thanatos disagreed.

"Thanatos, he's my brother," Andrina reminded him .

"I know that, but I'm not a man who will sit back and be run over," Thanatos informed her. "I will not allow Kristos to run you over either. You are a grown woman, and as such, you have the right to make your own decisions."

Andrina nodded. "Now, that I agree with, and he does tend to treat me as if I'm five sometimes." She sighed. "Although, he usually means well."

Thanatos was pleased that she didn't argue with him, so he gave her a gentle kiss before saying, "How about we ask each other a few questions, get to know a little more about each other, then I'll take you to dinner after a bit?"

Andrina was all smiling once more as she agreed, "Okay. I'll start with the fact that you mentioned having a daughter earlier."

"Erin."

"Were you married to her mother?" Andrina asked.

"*Ochi.* I had strong feelings for her mother, and I thought perhaps it might become love one day, but it did not. So, I suppose it just wasn't meant to be," he told her. "What about you, any serious boyfriends?"

"No. I was always shy, mostly because of my weight, and I suppose I tended to hide behind Kristos," she told him. "I did date a couple of men after high school was over, but neither relationship went past a few dates."

Thanatos hummed softly but stayed quiet.

"I am curious about something though, who are your parents?" Andrina questioned.

"My father is Erebus or darkness. My mother is Nyx, goddess of the night," Thanatos answered. "Is Kristos your only sibling?"

"Yes, he's it," Andrina murmured, "and he's a good man most of the time, Thanatos, he truly is. I think that if you and he would give each other a chance, you might become friends."

"Maybe," Thanatos agreed, feeling unsure. "I don't wish to be at odds with your family, darling, so for you, I will try my best to endear myself to your brother."

"Is Hypnos your only sibling?"

Thanatos laughed before he exclaimed, "Not by a

long shot! If you know anything about the gods and goddesses, you know they are a promiscuous bunch. So, there is Gerās, the god of old age; Nemesis, the god of retribution; Apate, goddess of deceit; Dolus, the god of deception; Charon, the boatman of souls. I have many more, but those are a few of them. Of course, you've met my twin, Hypnos, who is the god of sleep." He hummed in thought, then added, "There is also our sisters, the Keres, which are the daemons of violent death and disease. They are there to claim souls who died violently, whereas Hypnos and I come and take claim those who died peacefully. Although, I did recently take the souls of the men Ares killed because I was already there."

"Yes, I did remember that you are the spirit of nonviolent death," Andrina murmured as she rubbed his chest in a soothing circle. "The Keres tend to try and take souls in the most blood-thirsty way possible, correct?"

"*Nai*," he agreed. "Now, let us speak of other things. How about this? What is your favorite fruit?"

"Well, I'd have to say I like a lot of different ones," Andrina murmured, "but the mango would probably be my first choice."

So, the two of them spent the rest of the afternoon laughing and teasing each other as they learned random things about one another. At least until her stomach growled loudly, and Thanatos decided it was time to take her to dinner.

It was late by the time Thanatos took Andrina home. They'd gone to see a movie before having a late dinner, but he still wasn't ready to tell her good night, even though it was well after eleven p.m.

After dismounting his motorcycle and helping her get off, he pulled her close to him, his arms holding her to him gently. Her face was now lying against his chest as her arms wrapped around his waist. She hummed softly between her yawns as she encouraged him to sway slowly by moving her body.

So, as they swayed in an impromptu dance, he murmured, "I'm not ready for this evening to end, but I know you're tired."

Andrina's soft laugh was interrupted by a yawn. "Sorry, I can't seem to stop yawning, so I guess there is no denying I'm tired just to keep you here a bit longer."

"I will stay as long as you want me to, *o glykós mou peirasmós*," Thanatos murmured. When he felt her shiver, he smirked at her reaction. "Do you like me calling you, my sweet temptation?"

"You know I do," she whispered. "I also know you

would stay with me as long as I wanted you to tonight, and I like that about you. However, I won't ask it of you." Andrina raised her head, dropped her arms, and stepped slightly away from him. "I want you to know I had a lovely time with you today, Thanatos."

The smile left his face at her words. Drawing back slightly, he cupped her chin in his hand and said, "I hear a but in there. Have you changed your mind after hearing everything? Have you decided I'm not worth the trouble?"

"No! Please, don't think that Thanatos," Andrina said as she looked him square in the eyes. "I just think that a couple of days to let everything you told me sink in is in order. Thanatos, you laid a lot on me today about who and what you are. I need time to process all of it, and you know it's a lot."

Thanatos gave a resigned nod because she was right. He figured if he were in her shoes, he'd be wanting time to sort through everything also. He might not like it, but she deserved to process.

"Not only that, but you also told me you love me. We've only known each other for such a short time that it doesn't seem possible for you to love me already. Please, try and understand. I just need a little time."

Thanatos sighed and hugging her tightly, saying, "I don't like it because the thought of not seeing you for two days almost physically hurts me, Andrina. However, I will give you those two days because I would do anything for you. Remember one thing, Andrina, my feelings for you will not change. You are the one I have waited for, and I will not give you up without a fight."

Andrina nodded as she slowly, almost reluctantly, withdrew from his arms. Giving him a sad smile, she blew him a kiss before quickly turning and making her way up the driveway.

CHAPTER SEVEN

Once Andrina was on the porch, she opened the door to her house before she turned to lean against the door jamb. Glancing back, she watched as Thanatos mounted his motorcycle and spun out of the driveway. She stayed there, not moving until the taillights were gone, and she couldn't hear the roar of the bike anymore.

Feeling the pressure of tears welling up, she stepped back, closing and locking the door. Leaning her forehead on it, she breathed deeply, pushing the tears back before they could fall.

"So, you finally remembered where home is?" Kristos angrily snapped from behind her.

Andrina opened her eyes and blew out a breath as she turned her head to glare at him over her shoulder.

Kristos pointed at the clock that graced the wall of the entryway, causing her to glance over. Noticing it was almost midnight, Andrina internally cringed but still retorted back to him, "I remember perfectly well where I live because it has become apparent that I live under the thumb of an ogre."

Kristos snorted loudly, his arms crossed over his chest. "Being concerned about you does not make me an ogre. What do you see in that biker anyway? Honestly, tell me, I want to know."

Andrina felt the anger flow out of her as she pushed herself away from the door. "He makes me feel beautiful, Kristos. Even though he has his insecurities to deal with, he listens when I talk about mine and gives me encouragement that makes them disappear as if they were never there. He sees me, Kristos, not just my thick waist, but for who I am on the inside."

Kristos moved forward to pull his sister into a hug, whispering, "You are beautiful, Andrina, inside and out; you should never doubt that. I know some of my friends weren't always kind to you, and I'm sorry I let that happen."

"I love you, Kristos, you are my brother, and you have always been there for me," Andrina murmured. "Now I'm asking you to at least give Crusher a chance. He's a good man, and I want the two of you to at least try and get along."

"I love you too, Andrina, and because of that, I will give him a chance. However, if he hurts you, I will—"

Andrina laughed, pulling away from her brother to head for the stairs. Halfway up, she paused to peer over her shoulder and say, "I know, I know, you'll *attempt* to hurt him in return."

"It will be more than an attempt!" Kristos exclaimed. "I will succeed in the endeavor despite how freakishly large he is!"

Andrina just laughed and continued up the stairs as she answered, "Whatever helps you sleep at night, brother dear, whatever helps you sleep at night."

"Skull, where did you disappear to yesterday? Did I tell you that you could leave? Oh, wait, that's right, you didn't bother to ask, you just up and left," Zeus complained when Thanatos walked into the garage the next morning.

Thanatos stared blankly at the Greek god of the sky, wondering what he was on about. Finally, with a shake of his head, he continued to walk toward the stool he had placed in the corner for himself. Once he was there, away from the mortals working on vehicles, he sat down and crossed his arms over his chest. He then proceeded to glare at Zeus.

Zeus glared right back as he walked closer.

Thanatos let out a loud derisive snort and, in Greek, replied, "It isn't like you truly need me to be here. All I do is ramble around, try to look busy, and make the mortals extremely uncomfortable in my presence."

"You could watch the mortals work and try to learn something," Zeus shot back, also in Greek.

Thanatos could see how angry Zeus was getting by how he'd narrowed his eyes. The fact that his face was red and he had a vein pulsing his temple completed the look of fury. No, Zeus was not happy at all, but Thanatos didn't care.

"Oh, and why would I want to do that?" Thanatos questioned. "I have no interest in learning a mortal trade or in getting greasy. How about you go watch them instead?"

"Whatever," Zeus said with a negligent flip of his hand.

Thanatos blinked, stunned as all traces of Zeus's anger were suddenly gone.

"Now, why don't you tell me what I want to know," Zeus demanded. Leaning back against the wall, he crossed his arms over his chest.

"I went for lunch," Thanatos offered.

"Lunch doesn't take all day," Zeus snorted.

"Prophet mentioned that the two of you met a woman while you were out the other day, and it would seem the same woman came to see you yesterday."

Thanatos humorlessly chuckled when he realized what the conversation was truly about. Zeus was irritated that yet another of the gods had taken notice of a mortal woman. *Well, too bad for Zeus. I'm not going to stop seeing Andrina just because he has an issue with it.* So, he answered, "Yes, I left with a woman, a mortal woman, and we had a very nice afternoon and evening."

Zeus straightened up and moved in closer to where Thanatos sat. Leaning in, close enough to speak into Thanatos' ear and not be heard by anyone else, he demanded, "Stay away from the mortal woman, god of death. We've already had two go and fall for their charms, and we don't need you doing the same."

Thanatos got up from the stool, shoving it backward until it hit the floor, the sound echoing through the garage. He noticed some of the mortals had jumped at the sound. Then they turned around to see what was going on.

Now towering over Zeus by more than a foot, he glanced down and glared menacingly at him. He wasn't about to cower down like Zeus probably expected him to, not now, not ever.

Zeus continued to glare right back, not intimidated at all.

Thanatos decided right then he'd had enough of Zeus and his overbearing attitude for one day. So, turning on his heel, he headed for the door. Before he walked out, he tossed the words, "Too late, I've already fallen," over his shoulder. Then he strode swiftly out of the building to his motorcycle.

I'll head for Marlo's Diner and skip another day of work. Not going back to work today will give Zeus an actual reason to be irritated at me. Hmm, I believe that is the best I've had since yesterday when I skipped work to spend the day with Andrina.

Laughing to himself, he mounted his motorcycle and started it up. Thanatos made sure he laid rubber in the parking lot when he took off, heading for the diner.

———

Once inside Marlo's Diner, Thanatos sat in the far corner and stared out the window blankly after ordering breakfast. Ten minutes later, a plate appeared in front of him, a shaking hand holding it, and he glanced up. He gruffly murmured, "Thank you."

The waitress swiftly sat his plate down, gave him a nod, and left.

Thanatos sat, and as he ate, he contemplated what he wanted to do next. He was tired of being in the mortal world and was more than ready to go home. Perhaps it was time to pack it in and call it a day. He could always come back later if Zeus insisted on it.

What about Andrina? She asked for a couple of days to think about everything I told her. He took a sip of water. *Hmm, I suppose I could go home now and come back in two days. I just need the balance that home gives me. I've never stayed here in the mortal realm this long before.*

"So, this is where you run off to hide when things get tough?" a sweetly feminine voice said as someone slid into the seat across from him.

Glancing over, Thanatos found Cathy, the wife of Ares, sitting there. As he picked his fork back up, he replied, "Sometimes. So, what brings you here?"

"Well, a little birdy told me you stormed out of the shop and hightailed it down the road," Cathy answered.

"Mm-hm… interesting," Thanatos mused. "Who exactly is this little birdy? I didn't see Mad Dog anywhere this morning when I went in."

"No, it was Prophet actually," Cathy answered as she propped her chin in her hand, elbow on the table.

Thanatos raised his eyebrows at her answer, causing her to laugh.

The waitress walked over. "Can I get you anything, ma'am?"

Cathy glanced up. "A glass of tea would be great, thank you."

With a nod, the waitress turned to Thanatos, "More coffee, sir?"

"I'm good, thanks."

"Shocking, I know," Cathy said as the waitress walked away. "It seems Apollo's a bit worried about you because he believes the love plague has infected you."

Thanatos glared about the meaning behind her words.

With a laugh, she held up her hands in front of her and said, "Calm down and don't shoot the messenger. Those are Prophet's words, not mine."

"I highly doubt he's worried about me."

Cathy shrugged. "Does anyone know what goes on in his mind? I sure don't."

Thanatos shook his head as he took a sip of his coffee. "Infected. *Nai,* he did mention something the other day about me needing to stay away from him. Prophet still has it in his mind that falling in love with a woman is somehow contagious. I believe he fears he might catch it next."

"Well, he apparently heard you tell Tank earlier this morning that it was too late to warn you away from a woman," Cathy quietly mentioned as she folded her hands on the table and leaned close. "So, have you found a woman?"

Thanatos nodded as he answered, "I have and there will never be another who is as beautiful to me as she is. She is *peirasmé mou,* my temptation, and I couldn't be happier."

"Your temptation, huh? Like Irena is Hades' jewel, and I'm Ares' warrior woman?"

Thanatos nodded his agreement to her inquiry.

"Nice, gotta love those sweet names that just roll off the tongues of our local gorgeous Greek men," Cathy said with a breathy sigh and a dreamy look.

Thanatos raised his eyebrow at her.

After a short chuckle, Cathy leaned back in her seat, rubbing the chill bumps on her arms. "When do the rest of us get to meet this temptation of yours?"

Thanatos lowered his eyes to the table and his now empty plate. Pushing it away, the food he'd eaten, now a hard lump in his stomach, he replied, "I don't know. I laid a lot of information on her last night.

"Ah, you told her who you are, correct?"

Thanatos nodded. "I did. I didn't have much choice because of something that happened. Regardless, it caused her to say she needed a couple of days to figure it all out."

"Oh… that bites royally. I know how hard I took it

when Ares told me. Well, you were there, so I guess you do know. Still, I'm sorry to hear you have to go through it too."

"It had to come out eventually. The biggest thing is her brother doesn't like me much. I'm worried he'll talk her out of being with me, or at least try to. Anyway, I've decided to go home in the meantime."

Cathy nodded and hummed softly. "She has you all in knots, and you need the familiar. I can understand that, and no one would blame you if you went home. Now, how about you tell me all about her, starting with her name."

With a slight grin, Thanatos did just that, saying, "Her name is Andrina…"

Andrina paced across her bedroom floor, mumbling to herself as she brushed her hair. It had been two days since she'd seen Thanatos, and she was missing him something fierce. When she'd asked him to give her time, she hadn't thought about how hard it would be not seeing him at all for two days.

"Well, they do say that absence makes the heart grow fonder," she huffed as she came to a stop.

"Whose absence is making your heart grow fonder, Andrina?"

Andrina turned at the sound of her brother's voice coming from the direction of her open bedroom door. She gave him a slight smile as she answered, "Crusher's absence. I know you don't like him much, but I miss him a lot."

"It's true, and I don't like him. Nevertheless, I said I'd give him a chance, and I will," Kristos reminded her. He winked and teased, "He hasn't come around for two days though, so are you sure he feels the same as you do? Unless, of course, instead of going to work, you've been sneaking off to see him on the sly."

"First off, I know he feels the same way I do. Second, no, I haven't been sneaking around to see him; I truly have been going to work. Third, I asked him to give me time to think about some of the things he told me about himself. Which is why I haven't seen him for two days," Andrina admitted reluctantly, barely able to meet her brother's eyes.

She knew he'd find it odd that she'd defended Thanatos one minute, and practically in the next breath, she was talking about needing space from him.

I should have continued seeing him and getting to know him even better while I thought about what he told me. Doing so would have made a whole lot more sense than asking him to back off for two days. Andrina sighed to herself. *In hindsight, I realize this was not the best way to start a relationship with someone. What was I thinking?*

Kristos raised his eyebrows as he leaned against the door jamb and crossed his arms. "Oh, and what exactly did he have to say that would make you do that?"

Andrina walked across the room to lay her brush down on her dresser, thinking. She knew she had to be careful what information she gave out about Thanatos. The fact that he was a god wasn't her secret to give out; it was his. Regardless, she knew she had to tell her brother something, or he would never leave her alone. So, she answered, "Well, for one thing, he has a daughter."

"Does he have a wife to go with this daughter?" Kristos inquired as he straightened up, frowning harshly. "It's never a good thing to get involved with a married man, Andrina."

"Oh, come on, Kristos, give me a little credit! I know better than to go messing around with a married man."

"I should hope so, but lately, you have been acting out of character," Kristos said.

Andrina huffed as she sat down on her bed. "Maybe I have been acting different, just a little bit, but not to the point of being stupid."

"Fine, you still have a few brain cells," Kristos agreed. He laughed as she threw a pillow at him. He leaned, and it missed, hitting the floor next to him. "Seriously though, no wife?"

"No, I got the idea they never married. I'm not even sure if it was even a real relationship between Crusher and her." Andrina frowned thoughtfully.

"So, that was it? That's all you're concerned about," Kristos commented, his frown smoothing out a look of relief now on his face. Walking closer, he placed the pillow on the end of her bed. "Well, the way I see it if the woman isn't still in the picture, I honestly don't see a problem. Unless, of course, she pops up everywhere just to create problems in his relationships."

"No, nothing like that," Andrina denied. "There are other things he told me too, but they're things that I can't divulge to you because he asked me not to tell anyone."

"Secrets, Andrina? I didn't think we kept those from each other."

"My secrets? No, I don't keep those from you, but Crusher's secrets aren't mine to tell," Andrina informed him. Standing up, she walked around him to her dresser. Picking up her perfume, she sprayed a little on her wrist and neck.

How will Thanatos explain things to my family? It's not like they wouldn't eventually notice that he's different, if only because he won't age as we do. Have the two of us seriously thought this through? Is there any way for us to be together? Maybe there isn't, and we're both just fooling ourselves.

"Okay, you're right," Kristos commented, his voice pulling her from her thoughtful reflections. "It isn't your place to tell the secrets of others. My question to you is this, will knowing all his secrets cause you heartache?"

"No. What Crusher has confided in me about is mostly things about his past, his family," Andrina answered. It was only half the truth, but she hoped her brother wouldn't see right through her and realize it.

"All right. So, what are you going to do about missing your biker?"

Andrina laughed, watching her brother through the mirror and saying, "I guess I'll call him and see if he wants to meet up somewhere today. I asked him for two days, and it's been two days. The longest two days of my life, I think."

"What you should do, is have him come over and meet Mom, maybe for dinner," Kristos suggested.

"I suppose," she agreed, "Mom does need to meet him at some point."

"She does," Kristos agreed as he turned to leave.

"Hey, Kristos, do you think Mom would be scared of Crusher?"

Kristos turned with a frown.

Andrina bit down hard on her lip as he stared at her. She knew it was an odd question and was already regretting having asked him when he inquired, "Why would she be scared of him?"

"It appears that most women tend to be scared of him," Andrina answered. "I guess because he rarely smiles and because of his size."

"I can't answer for Mom because I don't know how she'll react," Kristos said. "I would suggest you mention his size and his permanent frown to her if you think it might be an issue. You know what they say, forewarned is to be forearmed."

Andrina nodded. "You're probably right; I should prepare her."

"I'm guessing the fact that you aren't scared of him is one of the things that draws him to you."

"It does help," Andrina said. "I would think it would be hard to have a relationship with someone if they flinched every time you drew close to them."

"Yes, I suppose it would," Kristos murmured. "Maybe that's why it didn't work out with the mother of his child."

"Perhaps," Andrina agreed as she watched her brother leave.

Grabbing her phone from her dresser, she took a deep breath and began to type a quick text to Thanatos. No time like the present to invite him to dinner.

If he says yes, I'll go and talk to Mom. Although perhaps

I should talk to Mom even if he says no. She needs to know about him because, at some point, they will meet.

With her finger hovering over the send button, Andrina took one more deep breath, and then she hit the little arrow icon. After sending the text, she sat back to wait.

CHAPTER EIGHT

Thanatos laid sprawled on his large bed on his stomach. He had his wings out and was flexing them slightly as he relaxed. He'd just gotten back from a short day trip to his home in the Underworld and was feeling a little more settled than he had been. He was still concerned about what Andrina would tell him, but there was nothing he could do about it until he heard from her.

His cellphone chirped from where it sat on his nightstand, and he raised his head. He reached out and picked it up, bringing it close enough to see he had a text from an unknown number. Curious who it might be , he clicked on the text icon to open it up.

"This is Andrina. Are you busy, or can you talk?" he read out loud to himself. He texted back with a pleased grin, with some difficulty because of his large fingers, that he did indeed have time to talk.

Laying it down on the bed in front of him, he waited. Not more than a minute later, the cellphone rang. Swiping the answer button, he put it on speaker and said, "Hello."

"Good morning, Thanatos," Andrina answered in a soft tone. "I hope you don't mind me calling you so early."

Thanatos hummed happily at the sound of her voice. "Good morning to you also, Andrina. It's good to hear from you, and it will never be too early because I would talk to you anytime, day or night."

"It makes me happy to hear that," Andrina said. "I will admit I was a little worried you might be upset with me since I asked for the two days."

"I might have been upset because I couldn't see you, darling, but I understood why you asked for the time," Thanatos solemnly told her.

"I will admit your words soothe my worry," Andrina told him. "So, moving on to the reason I called."

"And that is?"

"I want to invite you to dinner. I thought it might be a good thing for you and my mom to meet each other," Andrina answered.

The smile on Thanatos' face dropped, his brows

coming together in a heavy frown at her words. He'd
hoped to see her alone; he'd missed her and wanted to
spend time with her, just the two of them. *Why do I
need to meet her mom now?* Why *not later, after Andrina
and I have had a chance to bond a bit?* Needing to know
the answer to his internal question, he asked, "Why?"

There was a long pause before Andrina answered,
"I just thought that since Kristos has met you that
Mom should also."

"So, if your mother doesn't like me any more than
your brother does, then what? Is that the way you plan
to decide if you want to spend time with me or not?"
Thanatos asked, his insecurities rearing their ugly
heads and making his words harsh.

Thanatos had already decided that her mom
couldn't possibly like him. She'd probably feel the way
most women did and wish him out of her sight. He
might as well give up now. All it would take was a look
of fear on her mom's face, on top of the look of
distaste on her brother's, and she would quickly
decide he wasn't worth the effort.

"That is not it at all, Thanatos, and it hurts that you
would even think that about me," Andrina whispered.

Thanatos swallowed hard. He didn't want to hurt
Andrina, that was the last thing he wanted to do, but he
would be the first to admit his insecurities were almost
swallowing him whole right now. Still, he shouldn't

have taken it out on her. "I'm sorry, please forgive my terrible attitude, darling. I have missed you."

"I have missed you too," Andrina whispered back. "Thanatos, I want to be with you, and because of that, I would like for you to get to know my family. Kristos has promised to give you a chance, and I'm hoping the two of you will at least be civil toward one another, even if you don't like each other."

"I would do anything for you."

"That's good since I plan to meet your family after you meet mine," Andrina informed him. "This is how it works here in the mortal world; meeting the families is a significant part of any relationship."

Thanatos closed his eyes, unable to stop another shudder of worry from going through him. Other gods only had to glance a woman's way, and they were dropping at their feet in a swoon. All he had to do was get close enough for them to feel his chill, and they practically ran away screaming. He honestly wasn't sure if his heart could take the beating if Andrina turned on him because her family disliked him.

He knew most women listened to their moms, believed every word spoken by them. If her mom told her Thanatos wasn't worth it, he could lose her before he ever really had her.

If only she would have given me time to woo her, to bind

her to me, to make her feel as if she can't live without me. If she had done that, her mom's words wouldn't have as big of an effect on her as I fear they will.

"Thanatos? Are you still there?"

"Yes, I'm here," Thanatos answered. After taking a deep breath, he responded to her previous question. "I will come to dinner at your home. What time do I need to be there?"

"We usually eat around six in the evenings," Andrina answered with an excited voice. "I'm so glad you're coming over, Thanatos; I promise you won't regret it."

Thanatos gave an internal sigh as he murmured too low for her to hear, "I truly hope she is right, and I won't regret it." Then, in a voice loud enough for her to hear, he said, "Andrina, I need to know that no matter what happens with your mother that you will still give me, give us, a chance. Can you do that?"

"Thanatos, I know I've mentioned how much I like you, and it's a lot, believe me," Andrina soothed. "Sure, I won't lie, I'm hoping my mom will like you as much as I do. However, if she doesn't, it isn't going to change my feelings for you. Will it make it more complicated? Yes, but not impossible."

Thanatos let himself slump against the bed in relief at her words. They were a soothing balm to his wounded soul. "Okay, my darling. I will see you at six o'clock sharp."

"All right. Goodbye, for now."

"Goodbye," Thanatos agreed before ending the call.

Standing up, he stretched, thinking about how he now needed to find something to keep him busy until time to see his sweet temptation. Placing his phone on the bed, Thanatos took a deep breath and let it out slowly before retracting his wings.

He then headed to his kitchen for a drink. Pausing in the kitchen doorway, he saw his brother Hypnos standing at the kitchen counter.

"Good morning," Hypnos greeted him in Greek.

"Morning," Thanatos answered back.

Hypnos smirked then as he raised his coffee cup in a salute. "So, you're meeting the family for dinner tonight. Do you feel like a mortal yet, doing such common things?"

Thanatos opened his refrigerator and pulled out a cold bottle of water as he gave a humorless laugh. "No, I feel as if I'm going to my doom."

Hypnos gave him a confused look before he snorted and questioned, "Your doom? I thought you loved this mortal woman. Why would it feel like going to your doom? Thanatos, you should be happy that she thinks enough of you to want you to meet her family."

Thanatos watched his brother silently, waiting for

some words of wisdom. Hypnos had always been the smarter of them and seemed to know so much more than Thanatos felt like he did.

"The fact that she's inviting you to meet her mother should tell you something about her feelings. It should tell you how much she genuinely likes you, that she's ready to invest in this relationship. If she didn't see the two of you going anywhere, why waste her time introducing you to her mother? No, to me, this says she's ready to see where this is leading."

"Logically, I know you are right, but—" Thanatos paused as he tried to figure out the best way to explain himself. Throwing away his now empty water bottle, he headed for his living room.

Hypnos followed, and they sat down next to each other on the couch.

"You saw her brother's reaction to me, and you know how women react to me," Thanatos finally murmured. "What if her mom runs screaming or shakes in fear the whole evening? Do you seriously think that will make for a wonderful family reunion? Eventually, Andrina will begin to wonder if I'm worth it."

Hypnos shook his head sadly as he said, "I know your fears, and I know you've had to deal with them for a long time but give the woman a chance. If her daughter doesn't fear you, she might not either. You know there are a few mortals, though very few, that do not feel the chill of death."

"I know," Thanatos agreed, "and I believe her brother might be one of them. Either that or his anger overrides it somehow. For now, I should go and see if Zeus wants me to 'work' today."

Hypnos patted his shoulder before leaving in a cloud of gray smoke.

———

Andrina laid her phone down after speaking with Thanatos and heaved a heavy sigh. She had heard the worry in the tone of his voice and now wished she'd had them meet somewhere so they could have talked face to face. That way, she could have helped relieve his worries with hugs and kisses.

She understood where he was coming from; she had more than her share of insecurities, it seemed like sometimes. Andrina worried about what people thought of her due to her weight issues. Thanatos, of course, was concerned about how others perceived him because of his height. *Of course, the chills he gives them probably don't help much either. Poor guy, he got two strikes against him, and I know it hurts even if he does his best to hide it from everyone.*

Kristos had called Thanatos a freak the day they

met, and she figured he probably heard that a lot. He wasn't a freak though, at least not in her eyes. To her, Thanatos was unique and special. Sure, he was tall with a harshly solemn expression on his face most of the time, but deep down, he had a good heart. Sometimes a person just had to get past the outer appearance and see what was in the heart.

Hopefully, her mom wouldn't think the worst of him at first sight the way Kristos had. Maybe she would see the Greek god beauty that Andrina saw when she looked at Thanatos instead of the intimidating side of him. Maybe Thanatos would relax enough for her mom to see the gentleman's side she knew he had.

Andrina softly huffed as she walked out the bedroom door. She then began to grumble under her breath, saying, "That's a whole lot of maybes, making me unsure whether Thanatos stands a chance. *No*, that isn't so because I believe in him, and I believe in my mother's ability to see things rationally. On the other hand, Kristos tends to be arrogant and irrational, only looking at the surface. I love him to death, but he does have his faults." Walking quickly down the steps, she called out, "Mom, where are you?"

"In the kitchen," Mom answered back. She glanced up from her coffee cup when Andrina walked in. "Good morning."

"Morning, Mom. I have something I'd like to talk to you about," Andrina said as she took a seat.

Mom leaned back in her chair, questioning, "Oh, what would you like to talk about?"

"You know I've been seeing a guy named Crusher," Andrina began, and her mom nodded. "Well, I invited him to dinner, but there are a few things I'd like to tell you about him before he comes."

"You know you can talk to me about anything, and I definitely want to hear about this man of yours."

"I know," Andrina agreed as she crossed her hands on the table in front of her. "Well, you already know he's part of a motorcycle club," Andrina began. "You should also know that he's extremely tall, like over seven feet tall."

Mom's eyes widened, but she said nothing.

"He also tends to look quite grumpy, even when he isn't," Andrina mentioned. Pointing to her eyebrows, she added, "I think it's the thick eyebrows myself, but that's just my opinion."

Mom laughed lightly, causing Andrina to raise an eyebrow in question.

"Sorry, it just reminded me of something I saw on my social media recently," Mom said. "So, what you're saying is, he looks a bit like an angry cat?"

"No, Mother, he doesn't look like an angry cat," Andrina mumbled. She covered her face with her hand

and shook her head slowly. After a moment or two, she uncovered her face and saw the amusement on her mother's face. Realizing she'd been teasing, Andrina groaned, which cause her mom to laugh.

"Gotcha!"

Huffing, Andrina continued, "I find him to be quite beautiful, in a manly way, despite his thick eyebrows."

"Honey, thick eyebrows aren't the end of the world, and I promise not to hold them against him.

"Kristos would," Andrina grumbled under her breath.

"Good thing I'm not your brother then," Mom said. "Besides, have you seen some of the girls he's dated? He honestly has no right to talk about this man of yours."

"Thanks, Mom," Andrina said with a smile. "Anyway, he tends not to smile much, and a perpetual frown does tend to turn people off. Despite that, he has a good heart, and I think if you give him more of a chance than what Kristos did, I honestly believe you'll like him."

Mom reached over and took hold of Andrina's hand as she told her, "I will give him a chance,"

"Thanks, Mom."

"Andrina, you have a good heart, and if you like him, then you see good in him. So, despite your brother's feelings toward him, I'm more than willing to meet him."

"A lot of people take one peek at how intimidating he is and turn away, never taking time to know him," Andrina admitted. "Kristos called him a freak the first time he saw him, and I know it hurt Crusher."

"Your brother doesn't know when to hush most of the time. You should know better than to listen to most of what he said anyway, Andrina," Mom scolded with a heavy sigh. "So, what are you planning to fix for this fellow of yours?"

Andrina happily began to tell her mom what she thought would be good to have for dinner.

Andrina smoothed down the front of her blouse after she'd finished plaiting her hair and stared at herself in the mirror. She'd chosen to wear a cream-colored blouse with a squared neckline which was cut just low enough to show a bit of cleavage. It was long-sleeved and flared out from the band of lace just under her breasts to flow down over her hips. She loved the material's silky feel, and it always made her feel pretty when she wore it.

She'd then matched the blouse with a simple pair of black dress slacks, which slimmed her up slightly, but she still disliked how big her thighs were because of how snug the pants were around them. So, turning this way and that way, she scrutinized her thick waist and thighs from every angle, hoping she looked good despite her physical flaws.

Oh, how I wish they weren't quite so big, so noticeable. However, wishing wasn't going to magically change how much Andrina weighed in the next ten minutes, so there was no use whining about it. It was what it was, and that was that.

Taking another deep breath as she slipped her black flats on her feet, preparing to leave her room just as the doorbell rang. With a grin forming on her face, she took off out the door, jogging down the stairs, and hollered, "I'll get it!"

Just as she hit the bottom step, Kristos came out of the sitting room and shouted, "Not if I get there first!"

"Kristos, no," Andrina whined as she moved faster. She'd wanted to get a kiss from Thanatos before they joined her brother and her mom. *Stupid Kristos is going to ruin everything.* Somehow, she did manage to get to the door first and latched onto the doorknob when Kristos reached her.

"I know what you're planning, and as the man of this house, I can't in good conscience allow it to happen," Kristos said in an arrogant tone. Then he began almost laughing as he grabbed hold of her hand

and tried to pry it from the doorknob. With his other hand, he grabbed hold of her waist, trying to move her away from the door.

"Kristos, let go of me!" Andrina hollered.

"No, not until you let go of the doorknob," Kristos answered back, continuing to tug at her.

Andrina tried to use her body to push Kristos away; instead, all she managed to do was turn the doorknob. The door flung open from their movement, surprising her and Kristos both and sending them to the floor.

"Kristos," Andrina screeched, "now look what you've done!"

"It's your fault," Kristos grunted from under her. "You're the one running through the house to answer the door when I was perfectly capable of doing it. Now get off me, you're squishing my manhood, and I'll need it in the future."

Andrina was about to laugh and tell him it served him right when a sound of anger came from the doorway.

CHAPTER NINE

Andrina and Kristos stopped their bickering in shock at the sound of the low, slightly animalistic growl. They turned their heads, in sync, their eyes wide, to gape at the seven feet plus of pure rage standing there in the form of Skull Crusher.

Andrina noticed that Thanatos had his fists clenched as well as his jaw. His mouth was turned down in an angry frown, his eyebrows almost a single line above narrowed eyes, as he glared at her brother. She'd practically swear his eyes had flashed red for a moment as he tried to control himself. His nostrils flared as he took deep breaths.

Not sure what she should do to calm him, she whispered, "Crusher?"

His eyes moved from her brother to her. His gaze

softened somewhat, but the frown remained. In his unnaturally deep voice, he asked, "Are you alright?"

Andrina smiled when she realized his anger stemmed from his worry that she might be hurt. "I'm fine."

———

A gasp from further inside the house caused Thanatos to turn away from Andrina. He curled his lip back slightly as anger continued to pulse through him. He relaxed somewhat at the sight of a small woman staring at him; her eyes widened. She was a tiny woman, probably not much more than five feet tall, and looked like an older replica of Andrina.

There is no doubt in my mind that this is the mother of my sweet temptation.

Thanatos tried to relax, and stop the anger from moving through his body in waves because he didn't want to scare Andrina's mother. He was worried that the cold chill which naturally came from him, as body heat did from mortals, might be more potent in his anger. So, he took deep breaths, but he knew the only thing that would help him at this point was to have Andrina, his sweet temptation, in his arms.

Glancing down at Andrina and her brother, he saw they were both still frozen on the floor. He wondered if they had feared any slight movement from them would set off his anger again. With that thought in mind, Thanatos forced his fists to relax. In as soft a voice as he could muster, still slightly infused with anger, he murmured, "Let me help you up, darling."

He reached down and grabbed her around the waist with both hands and lifted her up and off her brother. Instead of placing her on her feet, he brought her up against him. Their eyes were now level, and her feet were dangling in the air.

Andrina's cheeks were pink, her eyes wide when they met his, and she murmured, "Good evening, Crusher."

"Good evening, my sweet temptation, I have missed you," Thanatos murmured to her in Greek. He knew the others would still understand what he said, but he needed the intimacy of using his mother tongue.

Andrina tilted her head slightly and raised her hand to brush it over his jawline. In Greek, she replied, "I missed you too. I was trying to get to the door first, so I could perhaps receive a kiss before I had to share you with the family." She gave him a self-deprecating smile before adding, "You see how that worked out for me."

Thanatos chuckled slightly, his body finally

relaxing completely. Speaking in English once more, he asked, "So, you are not hurt?"

"Just my pride," Andrina muttered with a huff.

"Hey, what about me? I ended up being your pillow," Kristos grumbled from behind Andrina as he stood up and dusted off his pants.

Andrina turned her head and scowled at her brother. "Well, it was your fault in the beginning. If you had just let me answer the door as any normal person would have…"

"I told you why I should be the one answering…" Kristos began only to be cut off by their mother.

"Children, we have company; let's act our age," their mother stated, stepping closer. "Stop with the bickering and let the man far enough into the house to close the door. The neighbors don't need to hear your squabbling."

"Yes, Mother," the twins answered at the same time.

Thanatos set Andrina on her feet after moving away from the door. He watched as she smoothed her hair back, her cheeks still slightly pink. It amused him slightly how Andrina and her brother both now had their heads down, their lips stuck out in identical pouts. They didn't want to be on their mother's bad side from the looks of it.

Kristos swiftly moved and closed the door making

sure Thanatos saw the quick glare he sent his way. Thanatos gave him an innocent smile in return because two could play this game. After all, he had a twin brother, and he knew all the tricks.

Their mother straightened her shoulders as she ran a hand over her hip. She then moved forward to stand in front of Thanatos. Holding out her hand to shake his, she cleared her throat and greeted him by saying, "Good evening, my name is Rachel Dukakis. I'm the mother of the twin terrors before you."

Thanatos gave a slight bow, taking Rachel's hand, which was slightly shaking, and kissing the back of it. He politely murmured, "My name is…" he paused, unsure what to tell her.

I honestly don't want to have her call me Skull or Crusher, but would it be wise to give her my real name? I did speak Greek, so she knows I'm Greek. Perhaps she won't think anything of my name. No, if anything goes wrong, she and Kristos shouldn't know my actual name.

"It's genuinely nice to meet you, Mrs. Dukakis. My name is Skull Crusher. Andrina has taken the liberty of shortening my name to just Crusher; if you would like to call me that, it would be fine."

Letting go of her hand, he stepped back to stand next to Andrina. Mrs. Dukakis was trying extremely hard to hold in the tremors coursing through her body when he'd been close, but he had seen them. Although she hadn't run, he could tell the chill of death she felt around him was making her uncomfortable.

"Please, call me Rachel." She twisted her hands together in front of her, possibly to stop them from shaking as she commented, "I do seem to remember Andrina telling me your name was Skull Crusher."

Thanatos nodded as he said, "That is my road name in the club. We don't give out our real names to anyone, and Tank frowns upon it."

"It's fine, I understand," Rachel replied. "Shall we go to the dining room now? Andrina worked tremendously hard on a meal for us. She informed me you were Greek, so we added a bit of Greek fare to the menu."

Thanatos glanced down at Andrina when he felt her grab hold of his hand. She smiled up at him, squeezing his hand before they followed her mother and Kristos into the dining room.

"Take a seat, everyone. Lisa, who is our housekeeper, will serve us," Rachel informed them.

Thanatos wanted to growl and hastily swallowed it back. *Great, another mortal to make uncomfortable with my mere presence. This night is genuinely beginning to seem like a mistake.*

Kristos held his mother's chair out for her. Thanatos did the same for Andrina. Then the men took their seats next to them.

Lisa, an older woman, possibly in her late fifties, stepped out of the door on Thanatos' left pushing a service trolley. She attended to Rachel first, then Andrina before she moved to the other end of the table to serve the two men.

Lisa never looked up from what she was doing, and Thanatos made sure she didn't see his face.

Thanatos figured since he was seated, he didn't have to worry about his height intimidating her. All he had to worry about was his facial expressions, the chill he could not change. He did notice the closer she was to him, the more she shivered as if cold, but her face never showed anything otherwise. Lisa was a professional; he had to give her props for that. Once she'd served everyone, she returned to the kitchen, and only then did Thanatos release a breath.

Rachel glanced across the table at Thanatos as she suggested, "How about you tell us a little about yourself, Crusher."

For long moments Thanatos stared down at his plate. He then cleared his throat as he glanced her way to say, "As I've mentioned, I'm in a motorcycle club. We call ourselves the Steel Chariots, MC, and I'm the enforcer for the club."

Rachel nodded as she stated, "I heard a while back, maybe a couple of years ago now, that a motorcycle club had come to town, so when Andrina mentioned it, it was no surprise to me. I also know what an enforcer is because my husband was in a club before we were together and told me a bit about it."

Thanatos glanced up, raising his eyebrows as he processed this new information.

Rachel smiled and picked up her fork before saying, "You weren't expecting that, were you?"

"Óchi," Thanatos agreed.

"So, any family?" Rachel asked. "Do they live close?"

"Most of my family is in Greece," Thanatos began.

"He has a twin brother, Mom," Andrina offered when he paused. "Kristos and I met him."

"Yeah, and he's just as big and ugly as this one is," Kristos muttered.

"Kristos! I did not raise you to be rude to people, especially not guests who have been invited into our home," Rachel scolded.

Kristos shrugged, seemingly unrepentant as he said, "I only speak the truth."

"Crusher isn't ugly, Kristos," Andrina huffed, her face turning red in anger, "and neither is his brother."

"He's probably ugly to everyone but you. A face only a mother could love," Kristos continued as he frowned, staring at Thanatos. "So, I guess I'd need to be female to understand what you possibly see in him or his brother."

"Err… Kristos!" Andrina began as she raised out of her chair slightly and leaned over the table, hand reaching out, ready to thump her brother.

Thanatos reached over and grabbed hold of her hand, gently pushing until she sat back down. He then lay her hand gently on the table. When she turned to look at him, he quietly reminded her, "I'm used to the insults, darling, don't worry about it."

"You might be used to it, but it still isn't right," Andrina informed him. "Besides, Kristos promised to give you a chance. Giving you a chance means being nice and not calling you names."

"I am giving him a chance, Andrina. I let him in the house, didn't I?" Kristos asked, widening his eyes dramatically.

"Kristos, grow up, please. And don't think for one moment we won't be discussing this attitude of yours later." Rachel sighed and rubbed at her forehead for a moment. Then she leveled her gaze back on Thanatos and asked, "What is your twin's name?"

Thanatos swallowed. *What do I tell her? Hypnos isn't exactly a common name. Wait, it might just be crazy enough to pass for an MC name, though, and she doesn't have to know he isn't in the club.* So, he answered, "His name is Hypnos."

Rachel's fork paused in midair as she stared at him.

Gently putting her hand back down, she questioned, "Hypnos?"

"Um, *nai*," Thanatos replied, nervous suddenly about the way she was staring at him.

Rachel's eyes narrowed, and she seemed to be thinking hard. Her steady gaze worried Thanatos because it made him think he'd made a mistake in giving his brother's name. However, Kristos and Andrina already knew his brother's name, so he couldn't precisely lie now.

"You're Greek, correct?" Rachel asked then.

Thanatos nodded, getting more nervous by the moment.

"You do know who Hypnos is in Greek mythology, right?" Rachel asked.

Once more, Thanatos nodded, his nerves causing his throat to dry. This was why he didn't interact with mortals daily. He left that to the bolder gods, too much stress.

"Then tell me something. Why did your President, Tank, I believe you called him, name your twin brother Hypnos, yet he didn't name you Thanatos?" Rachel questioned.

Andrina glanced at him, but her face, thankfully, gave nothing away.

Thanatos shrugged, the picture of calm outwardly even as he sweated bullets inside about what to say. He was a god, though; they practically learned how to lie at birth because it's just what they did. So, thinking fast, he answered, "Hypnos doesn't like guns, so he learned that thing with the neck that puts people to sleep…"

Kristos snickered behind his hand as he asked, "Would that be the Vulcan nerve pinch?"

Rachel turned her head slightly, her eyes narrowed and her lips pursed as she stared hard at Kristos.

"Nope, guess not. Oh, that's right, he's Greek, not Vulcan," Kristos muttered before covering his mouth to hide his snickering.

"Kristos, if you aren't hungry, you may leave the table," Rachel informed him.

Kristos suddenly stopped snickering and took a sip of his water.

Thanatos fought the urge to roll his eyes at Kristos and his comments. Instead, he calmly continued to explain as if he hadn't been interrupted. "It isn't exactly using hypnosis to put them to sleep, but close enough to warrant the name. I suppose that might be Tank's reasoning for my brother's name, but with Tank, one never knows. As for me, I've always been a rough and ready kind of guy, always ready to crush a few skulls in the name of brotherhood, subsequently, the name Skull Crusher."

"Mm-Hm… and is Tank also Greek?" Rachel asked.

"He is. All eleven of the original members are. We've added a few others who are from other places since we've been here though," Thanatos admitted reluctantly. He figured that eventually Rachel and Kristos would meet the rest of them, so hiding that they were Greek wouldn't be wise. He continued spinning his tale. "When we started, it was just a bunch of friends and a love of motorcycles. One day, Tank commented how we should become an MC, and it just snowballed from there."

I just handed her a line that it is nowhere near the truth, but it isn't exactly all lies either. Nevertheless, I'm hoping it will get her off the scent of whatever she thinks she smells.

Rachel hummed. She then began to eat, seemingly out of questions, at least for now.

Thanatos picked up his fork and began to eat also, feeling relieved there were no more questions. He was trying to be hopeful that all questionings would stop there, but one never knew because he'd found mortals to be a curious bunch by nature.

Roughly an hour later, dinner was finally over, and Thanatos sighed in relief. Now he could make his excuses and leave, the quicker, the better before Rachel started round three of the question brigades.

The questions hadn't stopped as he'd hoped they would after what he was calling the first round. Round one is the awkward questions about who he was. No,

Rachel had just changed her line of questioning and begun round two, which were even more uncomfortable. Round two consisted of the personal questions. Questions like, "Where did you say you met my daughter?" and "Are you just dating?" and "Do you think things might be a bit more serious than that?" From there, she had moved on to, "How do you make a living outside the MC?" and "Andrina is used to a certain lifestyle; can you support it?"

He had tried to stay stoic through it, but he could tell Andrina was highly embarrassed. At one point, Andrina had even told her mother she'd asked enough questions. That had not stopped her mother though. She'd just informed her daughter that it was her right to ask such questions, then she'd continued.

Kristos had sat, shaking his head and muttering under his breath. Thanatos thought he might have heard Kristos say something about how he would never bring a woman home, ever. Then there was something about his mother being beyond embarrassing and how he almost felt sorry for Crusher.

Andrina had sat, her face red, stuffing her face full of food and staring at her plate.

Thanatos had eventually begun to ignore the questions and refused to answer at all. He'd laid his hand on Andrina's thigh and squeezed gently in comfort. When she'd finally looked at him, he'd leaned over and whispered, "Your mother would put Tank to shame when it comes to grilling someone for information. Trust me, that's saying something because you will never meet a man nosier than he is."

Andrina had giggled and scooted back her chair as she said, "Mom, Crusher, and I have finished eating. So, since it's a nice evening, and I believe I'd like another ride on his motorcycle."

"You will do no such thing, Andrina!" Rachel exclaimed. "It's getting late..."

"Yes, it is, Mom," Andrina agreed. "However, I am a big girl and can take care of myself, so don't wait up." Then she practically dragged Thanatos from the room and out the front door after grabbing her coat and purse from the hall closet.

Something about how conveniently placed her coat and purse was made Thanatos think Andrina might have planned their escape ahead of time.

"Come on, come on, we need to hurry," Andrina told him as she almost pulled him down the driveway toward where he'd parked his motorcycle.

Thanatos managed to stay just enough behind her to enjoy her strut. Her hips swayed in a rhythm that only curvy women seemed to possess. Speaking in

Greek, he revealed, "Darling, you are such a sweet temptation tonight. I am thoroughly enjoying the view you are giving me."

Andrina turned to glance at him over her shoulder and grinned, not in the least bit embarrassed by his words. "Well, I will be enjoying the feeling of having my arms wrapped around your deliciously hard body soon. So, perhaps we'll be even with our fantasies."

As they stopped at his motorcycle, he wrapped his hand around her hair and gently tugged, encouraging her to tilt her head up and look at him. Once he was gazing into her eyes, and still speaking Greek, he murmured, "My fantasies include a whole lot more than either of those things."

Andrina's face did turn red then, and her breathing hitched as her heart began to pound. Also, in Greek, she whispered, "Take me home with you, Thanatos. I want us to be alone and uninterrupted so that we can partake in a few of those fantasies."

"Mm… and just how far into my fantasies are you willing to go, darling?"

"I don't know, probably not as far as you want to go, but I know my feelings for you are growing by leaps and bounds," she answered. "I also know I don't want to let you go tonight."

Thanatos let his eyes roam over her face and saw nothing but the truth on it. He could see she wasn't sure exactly where these feelings between them were going, but she was willing. He knew he was already in love with her and thought perhaps she might be almost there too. He desperately hoped she was, but at this stage, he would take what he could get. The only thing was his not wanting to let her go extended for much longer than for one night. He wanted her for the rest of his life.

"Let's just start with now and let later take care of itself," he suggested quietly.

When she nodded her agreement, he helped her onto his motorcycle. After he placed a helmet on her head, he seated himself and took off down the road.

CHAPTER TEN

Thanatos decided not to take her to his home, at least not yet. Instead, he drove a little way out of town to a road that wasn't much more than a dirt path. Once he'd turned onto it, he slowly drove up a short incline before pulling to a stop.

"This isn't your house," Andrina commented as she dismounted after him and removed her helmet.

"No, but it is one of my favorite places to go and find peace. At least it is when I'm here in the mortal realm," Thanatos murmured as he placed her helmet on the handlebar of his bike.

He took her hand and led her up the incline of the hill further into the woods. They walked a few moments before coming to a clearing that held big rocks. Leading her over to one, he sat, pulling her into his lap. He then leaned against the rock behind him.

"This is almost like a weird rock chair," Andrina murmured.

Thanatos watched her for a moment as she ran her hand over the smooth stone side, created as a perfect armrest. Kissing the top of her head, he informed her, "I know, I made it this way."

Andrina turned to stare at him, her eyes wide, as she asked, "You made a stone chair? Why?"

"As I said, I come here a lot to think," Thanatos said softly, running his knuckles over her soft cheek. "I wanted someplace to sit instead of on the ground, so I placed these rocks here. I placed other rocks around it, just to make it seem more natural if someone were to come across it."

"Well, I like it," Andrina informed him before giving him a quick kiss on the lips. "So, why did you bring me here instead of taking me to your home?"

Thanatos hummed softly before saying, "As I said, this is one of my favorite spots, so I wished to share it with you. I can find peace in the beauty and solitude of this place when the glances I receive from the mortals become too much. The first day we met, you met Apollo also, do you remember?"

"Apollo? Oh! Prophet. Yes, I remember."

"Well, as soon as you turned your gaze to him, my thoughts turned dark because I feared you would never glance my way again," Thanatos said, giving her another glimpse of his insecurities.

"Why wouldn't I look your way? You are beyond gorgeous to me, Thanatos, and I have no problems with how tall you are, even though you tower over me greatly," she told him with a soft giggle.

"Because all women are in awe of his golden beauty," Thanatos informed her. "He knows he is handsome, and he uses it to his advantage. All the boy has to do is smile, and the women practically fall at his feet."

"Well, not this woman. Apollo's golden locks do nothing for me," Andrina told him. Reaching up, she ran her fingertips through the slightly longer hair on the top of his head, tugging slightly before dropping her hand back to lay on his shoulder. "I like your dark, bad boy vibe."

"That's good to know," Thanatos told her with a smile as he hugged her close. "Seriously, that's excellent news because I don't see my image changing anytime soon."

Andrina laughed and agreed, "No, I don't suppose it will."

Thanatos was silent, thinking. Then he suggested, "How about we get to know each other even better."

"That sounds like a good idea. So, what would you

like to know first?" Andrina asked, watching him, her eyes wide.

He hummed softly. "What was your childhood dream?"

Andrina laughed, her whole body shaking as she inquired, "Are you sure you want to know?"

"*Nai.*"

"Okay, just remember, you asked for it. When I was about five, I decided I wanted to be king of a lion pride. I had been to the zoo, and I saw how sad the lions there seemed to be. I think there were five or six of them lying around. I remember thinking how filthy their cage was with lots of dirt and cement, but hardly any grass. I decided right then I needed to free them all, put them in our back yard, which and lots of grass and no cement, and declare myself their king to them. Well, I would declare myself king *after* magically transforming myself into a lion," Andrina explained as she laughed.

Thanatos threw his head back and laughed with her. When their laughter had calmed, he asked, "Why a king though, why not queen?"

"Because the mane on the male lion is awesome, of course," Andrina informed him haughtily. "Kristos told me I couldn't be a lion though, much less the king of them, and broke my little heart. He told me I could probably be a monkey since I was so good at climbing trees. I told him I didn't want to be a monkey and started to cry. Kristos hugged me and told me that was okay because he loved me just the way I was." She sighed and lay her head against his chest before saying, "Kristos and I used to be so close when we were little. I don't know what happened."

"You grew up and became independent," Thanatos said. "It happens to us all."

"I suppose, but sometimes I miss my brother," Andrina whispered, "even when he's in the same room."

Thanatos just held her close and rocked her slightly for a moment as he pulled the rubber band from her braid. He loosened the plait before running his fingers through it from root to tip. The silence lasted for quite some time, but it was a peaceful kind of silence that spoke of their contentment in each other's company.

Andrina cleared her throat a bit before asking, "So, what was your childhood dream?"

Thanatos gave a humorless laugh, "I had no child-hood dreams because I always knew why I was here, Andrina. It's one of the perks, or curses, depending on how you want to see it, of being a god. Your future is mapped out for you already, and there is no escaping it. As I grew older, I dreamed of having someone to hold and to love for all time. That didn't work out well the first time, but I did get my beautiful daughter out of it, so I suppose it wasn't a complete failure. Now though, I have you, and I hope with all my heart we work out."

Andrina stared up at him, and those big green eyes seemed to go past what he let everyone see, deep into his black soul. Her hand came up and cupped his cheek, and Thanatos held his breath, waiting to see what she would say.

Softly she said, "I want us to work out too, Thanatos. In the length of time I've known you, you have wormed your way into my heart, and I like having you there. I don't want you to go anywhere and find that feeling with someone else."

"I like having you in my life too, and I have no plans to go anywhere without you," Thanatos whispered back. He kissed her then, with all the feelings he had inside for her.

Slightly breathless, they finally broke apart, and she whispered, "Oh, and I quite enjoyed your twist on the truth you told Mom."

"About the club or me?"

"Both. Although, you might have to tell Mom the truth one day."

"We will cross that bridge when we get there," Thanatos told her. He knew, however, that telling her mother most likely would never be an option for him.

Then they continued their lively conversation, enjoying a few heated kisses in between topics. They talked through the night before, silently enjoying the sunrise. Next, they continued to speak until Andrina's words began to slur, and she went completely silent as sleep claimed her.

Thanatos then took them to his home, using his godly power of disappearing in a cloud of gray smoke. Once there, he placed her on the bed in his guest room and returned for his motorcycle. After bringing it home, he stripped down to his boxers and climbed into his bed, wishing he was with Andrina, and quickly drifted off to sleep.

Andrina stirred, stretching, and yawning as her eyes fluttered open. She felt warm and comfy, surrounded by a strange heat. As her eyes completely opened, she frowned at the wall in front of her. It wasn't her bedroom wall because it was a light gray, whereas her walls were pale blue. The room was also much darker than hers would be. With those realizations also came the feeling of weight over her chest and hardness under her head.

Her heart rate picked up as she glanced down at herself, and she couldn't stop the gasp that left her. She had a man's arm laying under her head, another arm over her, just under her bosom. The tattooed sleeve on the left arm soon had her relaxing and the frown leaving her face because she now knew it was Thanatos.

The frown quickly returned when she began to wonder how she'd even gotten into his bed. *The last thing I remember is the sunrise. How did we get here?* A quick peek under the edge of the cover showed she was only wearing a bra. *For that matter, why am I only wearing my bra? And I am in desperate need of a bathroom.*

Thanatos moved slightly behind her, his breath moving the hair on her neck sent a shiver down her spine. He hummed slightly before taking a deep breath and murmuring, "*Kaliméra*, Andrina, it's about time you woke up."

"Good day to you also, Thanatos," Andrina answered. "Would you like to tell me how we ended up here and why I have no shirt on?"

He chuckled and murmured, "Hey, you're the one who removed your clothing, not me. I brought you to my house because you were sound asleep. I then put you to bed in the guest room before going back to get my motorcycle. When I returned, you were still asleep, so I went to bed too. When I woke up around nine, I came in here to see if you might be awake..."

"What time is it now?" Andrina butted in to ask. She felt him moving behind her before he answered.

"It's just a few minutes after ten."

"Okay, continue."

He chuckled, and she felt him kiss the top of her head. "When I came in, I found your clothes laying on the floor next to the bed. Your covers were hanging off the end of the bed, so I was a gentleman and covered you back up. I then placed your clothes neatly in that chair next to the bed."

Andrina didn't remember removing her clothes but shrugged because it was too late to be crying over it now. Instead, she murmured, "And you decided to crawl into bed with me?"

"I hated to wake you up, so yes, I laid down with you," he agreed. "Please notice, Andrina, I'm laying on top of the blanket."

She huffed and muttered, "I need to use the bathroom."

"It's the door right in front of you," Thanatos told her. "There is an extra toothbrush on the counter, and if you would be more comfortable in something besides what you were wearing last night, I put a T-shirt on the counter for you also."

"Thank you," Andrina whispered as she turned slightly to kiss his cheek.

She waited for him to get up and leave the room,

noting that he was only wearing a pair of low-slung jogging pants. She watched the muscles in his back ripple with every move he made walking across the room before he closed the door behind him.

Moving quickly, she made her way across the room to the bathroom, closing the door behind her. She sighed with relief when her bladder was empty, then washed her hands and brushed her teeth before pulling the black T-shirt over her head. She laughed softly at her reflection in the mirror on the back of the bathroom door because the shirt was so long it fell to her knees.

Walking out of the bathroom, she found Thanatos had returned. He was lying on the bed, flat on his back. He had one arm tucked under his head and was frowning at his cellphone. Moving across the room, she propped pillows up against the headboard before stretching out next to him. Once she was comfortable, she let out a tired sigh.

Thanatos lay the phone aside and turned his head to smile at her. "Do you feel better now?"

"I do, thank you, although I'm still tired," she murmured as he turned sideways to lay his head in her lap. She had to smile when she saw how his legs now hung off the edge, yet he didn't seem to mind.

"Well, we did stay up all night, and you only slept for roughly three hours. Sleep means extraordinarily little to me, but I know most mortals need at least eight hours."

"True," she agreed as she stared into his dark eyes and ran her fingers through his messy hair. "Hey, do you remember me telling you about the big party my mother throws for our birthday every year?"

He nodded, watching her silently.

"Well, I was hoping you would go with me," Andrina said nervously.

Andrina waited for his answer as a dark look crossed his face. Thanatos turned his head so he wasn't facing her but the wall instead. The expression she'd caught a glimpse of before he'd turned had given her a chill down her spine, and she wondered if that was the look he said tended to send people running from him. It didn't scare her, but it did confuse her because he had never looked that way in her presence before, not even when Kristos had made him angry.

Andrina was curious as to why he would gaze at her that way. So, she inquired, "Thanatos, why do you look like that?"

Thanatos took a deep breath and let it out slowly before answering, "Look like what?"

Andrina gently cupped his chin with her hand and turned his head, so he faced her once more. Softly, she answered, "I'm not exactly sure what kind of expression it was, although I do wonder if it might be the one that sends others in the opposite direction from you. It is a dark look that caused chills to run down my spine."

Thanatos pulled her down and kissed her, closing his eyes and, in a whisper, begged, "Please don't fear me, Andrina, you are the light in my dark world of death. You have no reason to fear me, for you are the one who holds my heart in her hands."

"I don't fear you, Thanatos, but I do wonder what brought it on," she murmured. "I only asked you to come to my birthday party."

Thanatos opened his eyes, holding her gaze once more as he said, "Darling, you need to understand, I'm not like the other gods. When Zeus walks into a room, women swoon, and the men turn into a herd of jealous swine wishing they were him, as it is with most of the gods. They are beautiful beings that demand respect and strike awe in the hearts of the mortals with their beauty.

"I, on the other hand, strike fear in the hearts of mortals. I am the god of death. My aura is almost as black as the heart of Ares, the god of war. Mortals tremble in my presence because of who I am, even if they don't understand why. It isn't the expression on my face, or my towering height, not really. No, it is what I make them feel, the chill that fills them when I'm near."

"In other words, somewhere deep inside their psyche is the knowledge that you are Death. They just don't acknowledge it?"

"Something like that," he agreed. "They feel the chill of death when they come in close contact with me, and it scares them."

"Why don't I feel that? I feel no cold when you are near me, only warmth and a need to be closer to you."

Thanatos sat up and leaned against the headboard next to her. He reached over, cupping her neck, and pulled her closer until she was leaning against his chest. She snuggled into him with a soft sigh, kissing him on the chest.

"Because you are mine. The *Moirai* have blessed me with you, just as they blessed Hades and Ares with mortal women. Those women do not fear them, even though they know exactly who and what they are. I believe the *Moirai* knew it would take special women to turn the head of those two and keep their attention because many mortal women have tried and failed to do so.

"As the god of the Underworld, and as the god of war, their hearts are black, yet still, the *Moirai* were able to find them good matches, women who love them more than life itself. Seeing them fall in love gave me hope, hope I found in you the day we met," he concluded.

They lay silent for a long moment, content. Thanatos began to finger-comb Andrina's long hair as she drew shapes on his chest.

Eventually, he sighed and said, "I believe our union is blessed because the *Moirai* brought us together. When I am with you, all you see me as is a man. You don't see me as a god. Does that make sense?"

Andrina nodded and said, "It does. When we're together, you allow yourself to be you because you don't feel as if you have to prove yourself to me continually."

"That is exactly it," he agreed. "When I'm with the other gods, I dare not drop my guard lest I say or do something one of the gods will hold against me later."

"Do the gods feel the chill of death when they're around you?"

"No. The gods are immortal and don't feel such things," Thanatos answered.

"Kristos doesn't seem to feel it, maybe because we're twins," she suggested.

"I suppose that is a possibility. Or it could be because Kristos is usually too full of anger to notice anything else when I'm around," Thanatos reminded her.

"That is so true," she agreed with a hint of laughter in her voice. "I think Mom did."

"As for your mother, she's female, and I think you

are only the second one I've ever come across who does not feel it."

"Is the first one your... ex? Or baby mama? I'm genuinely not sure what to call her," Andrina whispered.

Thanatos chuckled softly and kissed the top of her head. "I suppose baby mama works because she didn't stick around long after Erin was born."

Andrina sighed, saying, "Okay, it works for me."

CHAPTER ELEVEN

Andrina stayed silent for a long time before she finally glanced back up at him, biting her lip. Finally, giving a soft huff, she said, "So, back to my question from earlier. My party, I'm guessing you don't want to go to it, which is why you gave me a dark look. Is it because too many mortals to feel your chill and become uncomfortable?"

"That is one reason, but regardless of that, I will go because you have asked," Thanatos informed her. "However, I fear, as you have said, it will make everyone there uncomfortable. No matter how hard I try to control it, Andrina, the mortals will feel the chill of death with me that close to them. It won't exactly put them in the party mood. The best I can do is stay on the sidelines where they won't feel it as strongly as they would if I were right next to them."

Andrina let her gaze drop to his chest as she whispered, "Is it terrible that I still want you to be there? Even though I understand what you are saying, it doesn't lessen how much I want you to be there, Thanatos. I go to the parties because my mom plans them for Kristos and me, but I never enjoy them. Usually, I try to stay under the radar because most of the guests don't want to have anything to do with me."

"Then why does your mother make you go?"

"Mom doesn't know how badly some of them treat me," Andrina whispered her answer. "When Mom and Kristos are around, his friends gush about me. They also speak very highly about me if they think someone might hear them. It's all so sickening."

"Then why have you not told her or your brother how those people treat you? I don't understand why you would put yourself through that every year just for a party?"

"Because I don't want them to know how much of an outcast I am," Andrina admitted with sadness. With tears flooding her eyes, she lifted them and connected them with Thanatos' dark eyes. "I tried for years to be accepted by classmates and those in our social circle, but it never happened. Now I sit back and avoid them all, thankful I don't have to be around them and deal with their pettiness daily. None of their opinions about me matter anymore, Thanatos; I'm so over trying to be someone I'm not. There are only two opinions that have mattered to me for a long time: my mother and Kristos. They matter to me because I know they love me and only want the best for me, which doesn't include ridiculing me over a few extra pounds."

"They love you, Andrina. Of course, they wouldn't criticize you. That alone shows me they wouldn't want you mistreated by others," Thanatos said.

Andrina shrugged and said, "No, they wouldn't want that for me, that's true. However, I know it would hurt them to know that they didn't see it going on practically under their noses. I don't want to do that to them."

Thanatos softly grunted but decided, in the end, it wasn't his place to tell her what to do. No, all he could do was support her from here on and hope she would change her mind about telling her family. So, with that in mind, he told her, "Fine, I will go to your party. Please do not be upset when I stay mostly at the sidelines. Just having me in the same room as the mortals will cause them to be slightly uncomfortable, but the further I am from them physically, the less noticeable it will be. I have learned that it does somewhat help. Trust me on this."

"I believe you, Thanatos, and I'm not bothered by you doing what you need to do. Regardless of that, it makes me extremely happy that you're going to be there with me," Andrina told him. "Now, how about you take me home? Oh! Home, what will my mom say when she realizes I was gone all night?"

"It's early yet, and I can take you home in a way that nobody will know you weren't home all night," he murmured. "Unless, of course, someone decided to check in on you during the night."

"I'm too old for my mother to come to my room and check on me, Thanatos," Andrina informed him with a laugh. "Well, honestly, I'm old enough to be out overnight too, I suppose. I'm just used to telling Mom if I'll be out and having not done that last night is simply weird for me."

"I understand, and I do seem to remember you telling her not to wait up."

"I did, didn't I," Andrina mused. "Maybe she read between the lines and figured I wouldn't be home then."

"Perhaps so," he agreed. "I was thinking more on the lines of your brother. I wouldn't put it past him to check and make sure you were safely in your bed."

"Hm... I didn't think of that. Kristos might check on me since he doesn't trust you yet, even though he said he'd give you a chance."

"He is a good brother to watch out for you, even if

he does quite annoy me," Thanatos softly said before pulling her in for a kiss.

Then, while he had her, lost in his kiss, he returned her to her home in a cloud of grayish smoke.

Andrina opened her eyes to find herself suspended in midair, held by Thanatos, who was standing in the middle of a room when he broke their kiss. She blinked, then blinked again because they now were in a bright sunlit room instead of the darkened bedroom she had been in just a moment ago. Her mouth dropped open as she stared at the laughing man in front of her. "How... you...?"

"I'm a god, remember?"

"Of course, I remember, silly man!" Andrina exclaimed. "Nevertheless, that doesn't explain how I suddenly ended up here, in my bedroom while you kissed me."

"You ended up here the same way I'm about to leave you because I hear someone outside your door," Thanatos explained to her before giving her a quick, chaste kiss and placing her feet on the floor. He then disappeared in a puff of grayish smoke, leaving her standing alone in the middle of the room.

Andrina stared at the spot where Thanatos had been standing, the smoke now completely gone as if it had never been. She couldn't seem to wrap her mind around what she'd just seen, even though

Andrina knew she *had* seen him vanish in a cloud of smoke.

"Andrina? Are you awake?" Mom called out from the outside of Andrina's bedroom door.

The sound of her mom's voice yanked her mind back into the present. So, she quickly made her way over to her bed and scrambled under the covers to hide the fact that she was only wearing a t-shirt and called out, "Yes, Mom, I'm awake."

The door opened, and her mom stuck her head inside to say, "I wanted to talk to you before your brother had a chance to."

Andrina nodded and sat up, propping herself against her pillows as she asked, "Sure, Mom, but about what?"

Mom sighed as she came in, closing the door. She then took a seat on the side of the bed, saying, "I wanted to talk about Crusher and how... odd he is. Andrina, Crusher seemed to skirt around most of the questions I asked him about himself at dinner. This bothers me because it left me with more questions than he answered. He never did tell us his real name, even though I hinted more than once for him to do just that. His excuse that his president, Tank, doesn't like them to just doesn't wash with me. We are your family, and if he's serious about you, there shouldn't have been a problem with him telling us. I am perfectly capable of calling him by his road name in public, should I see him there."

Andrina had no answer to give her mom. She knew this was her mom's way of finding out his name from her, or at least to see if she knew his name. The thing was, she couldn't tell her his name was Thanatos without raising even more questions. That would lead to her divulging secrets that he didn't want her to reveal to anyone.

"I also get a strange vibe from him, more like a cold chill really," Mom continued when Andrina stayed silent. "I honestly don't like how being around him makes me feel, Andrina. That is why I must agree with your brother when it comes to you dating this man. I don't think you should see Crusher anymore because there is something about him that isn't right."

Andrina sat straight up in the bed as she indignantly huffed, "Mom! I'm a grown woman, twenty-three years old, with a mind of my own, and if I wish to see Crusher, I will see him. It's not like you can stop me from seeing him."

"You're right, and I can't stop you. All I can do is suggest that you seriously think about this…"

"I have thought about it, and I know that I love him, really love him, and he loves me too," Andrina said, a little calmer.

"Andrina, you barely know him, so I very much

doubt it's love you feel for him. It's most likely that since he's the first man who has shown you any real interest in quite some time, you've developed a bit of a crush," Mom continued as if Andrina had said nothing. "If you stop seeing him, I'm sure these feelings you have will fade, and…"

"No, no, no, Mother! The feelings I have for him won't fade because this isn't a teen crush I have on him. It's love," Andrina argued as she stood up from the bed. "Nor will I stop seeing him. In fact, I invited him to my birthday party."

"You feel that strongly about him?" Mom whispered as she also stood.

"I do to the point that I believe fate brought us together, and I refuse to give him up," Andrina stated firmly. "We just clicked that first moment, and the feeling between us only grows stronger each time we're together."

Mom let out the breath she seemed to have been holding as she reluctantly agreed, "Okay. If Crusher is truly the man you want, then I won't stand in the way of that."

"Good."

"Just know that I'll be watching him closely," Mom stated before leaving the room.

"Watch all you want, but it isn't going to change

anything," Andrina murmured to herself as she watched her mom leave the room.

Turning abruptly, she walked into her bathroom, and once inside, she closed and locked the door behind her. Leaning her forehead on the door, she let out the breath she'd been holding. She didn't think she'd ever stood up to anyone the way she just had her mom. Deep in her heart, though, she knew that Thanatos was worth fighting for. Their love was worth fighting for, so if she had to fight, then that was what she would do.

———

Thanatos walked into the shop later that morning and glanced around. Not seeing any of the other gods, he was about to walk out when he heard his name spoken. Turning, he saw the mortal, Jim, standing next to a car. Walking over, he said, "Morning, Jim."

"Morning, Skull," Jim said with a grin.

Jim was a middle-aged man, probably only forty, if that. Thanatos had learned his name when they'd began speaking after Apollo's meltdown. Jim was one of the few men who didn't act uncomfortable speaking with Thanatos. The rest of the men tended to steer clear of him unless they just had to talk, and even then, they quickly left his presence afterward.

"Are you the only one here so far? I know I'm early, but I would have thought the rest of the crew would already be hard at work so they wouldn't suffer the wrath of Tank," Thanatos said as he glanced around the empty mechanic bay.

"Aw, that pussy cat? No need to worry about him," Jim teased with a glint of humor in his eyes. Everyone knew to stay clear of Tank and his rages.

Thanatos laughed and shook his head at the mortal's sense of humor.

"I'm a few minutes early. Since I have no ol' lady, home is a lonely place," Jim admitted. "Speaking of women, I saw the pretty girl who she came by to see you. Should we be listening for wedding bells soon?"

Thanatos chuckled and leaned on the truck that Jim was working on as he said, "I'm hoping for that. I believe she is willing, now if I can just get her family on board with it."

"Ah... family," Jim muttered. Then propping an elbow on the frame of the car, he gave Thanatos a solemn look, saying, "Don't let family stop you from being happy. I let my father dictate who I should and should not be with and ended up a heartbroken young man. I did end up marrying later on, but she wasn't the one I genuinely loved, and she knew it. She divorced me after only three years."

Thanatos stood, deep in thought, as Jim went back

to work. *Will her mother and brother try and keep us apart? Kristos did say he would give me a chance, but her mother, I'm not so sure about her. I remember the suspicious glances she continued to bestow on me throughout the meal, although she tried to hide them. I suppose time will tell what happens, but I'm not willing to give Andrina up. No, she is mine, my temptation, and I will not give her up so easily.*

"Skull!"

The shout from across the bay had Thanatos shaking his thoughts away as he glanced over.

It was Apollo, and he had an annoyed expression on his face as he walked over.

Thanatos frowned, his eyebrows pulling together and his eyes narrowing into irritated slits. *What is wrong with Golden boy now?*

"There you are," Apollo began. "Where have you been?"

"Around. Why do you ask?" Thanatos asked.

Apollo glanced over at the mortal; he then made a "follow me" movement with his head as he walked away.

With an apologetic shrug to Jim, Thanatos followed Apollo toward the backdoor exit.

Apollo led the way outside, murmuring, "I wanted to talk to you, Thanatos."

"What did you wish to talk to me about now?" Thanatos asked, not bothering to hide his irritation as they walked outside and around the building.

Apollo turned toward Thanatos with a frown of his own. Then, switching to Greek, he asked, "Are you still seeing that mortal?"

Leaning against the building, Thanatos crossed one leg over the other, hands now deep in his pockets. Giving Apollo a smirk, he also switched to Greek to answer, saying, "As a matter of fact, I am. Why are you jealous because you haven't found a mortal of your own? Lighten up, Golden boy; you've had your fair share of women. There is no use for you to be jealous of me having just the one."

"First off, I'm not jealous of you or anyone else," Apollo snarled back in Greek. "Second, yes, I've had my fair share of women, even a few mortal ones, but they weren't anything serious. You, on the other hand, seem to think this mortal is the love of your life!"

Thanatos raised his eyebrows at Apollo's audacity as he asked, "Oh, and how do you know that's what I think?"

"You have the same gleam in your eyes when you talk about her that both Hades and Ares get when they see their women. I still can't believe they tweaked the women's mortality so they would live longer," Apollo huffed. His shoulders then drooped as he turned to stare off into the distance. "Why did we even come here, Thanatos? Were we not happy enough on Mount Olympus?"

"I rarely go there," Thanatos murmured, only to have Apollo turn and glare at him. He held his hands up in surrender before he continued, "However, to answer your question, I highly doubt Zeus gave any of us much of a choice in coming here."

"True. Zeus does tend to make it sound as if you have a say when you honestly don't."

"Regardless, my idea when we first came here was to use it as a way to relieve a bit of my boredom. My life tends to be tedious and without much excitement. So, even though I'm here a lot, I've never stayed long enough to learn much about the mortal realm. So, I'll also admit to being curious."

"So, you came because you were curious!" Apollo ranted as his glare returned, his face now bright red with anger.

Thanatos wasn't bothered by the anger, knowing Apollo wouldn't do anything to him. So, he just shrugged again but said nothing.

Apollo breathed in deeply several times, which seemed to calm him. He admitted, "It's true, Zeus didn't give me a choice in coming here. He wanted a certain number of us to be here, and he knew Artemis wouldn't come without me and that Hera would ask her. So, Zeus threw a few threats around to make sure I came. He told me how much fun it would be and that it was a privilege to be "asked" to join one of his games," he snorted, crossing his arms, as he stared into the distance. "After he said that, I figured I had little choice but to come. I have to say, it isn't anything like I thought it would be, so I mostly try and stay out of his way."

"You only stay out of his way if you aren't sneaking around and snitching on the rest of us."

"I don't snitch. Zeus just tends to ask me a lot of questions," Apollo muttered.

Thanatos couldn't help but notice how Apollo refused to meet his eyes when he said it.

"Well, be that as it may, you can either make the best of it or stew in your misery," Thanatos informed him. "I prefer to make the best of it, and I'll admit I have enjoyed the Harley I bought. Riding with the wind blowing around me, the feeling of freedom I get from it, I relish it immensely."

Apollo grinned as he turned to face Thanatos. Still speaking Greek, he admitted, "I enjoy that as well. I don't care much for the fancy riding boxes the mortals call automobiles, but the motorcycle, I like it."

Thanatos straightened from where he was leaned

against the wall and stretched. "So, are we better now? I think we had better get to pretending that we're doing something before Zeus realizes we aren't. I don't feel much like being yelled at today."

Apollo frowned before he said, "I'm curious about one more thing, Thanatos."

Thanatos paused before leaving to glance back at Apollo and ask, "Oh, and what are you curious about?"

"Having spent quite a bit of time with you in recent weeks, I've noticed something. It seems to me as if most of the mortals tend to avoid being anywhere close to you," Apollo began. "Why is that?"

Thanatos turned his back on the younger god. He then replied with a question of his own, asking, "Have you ever heard the saying, I can feel the chill of death as it comes for me? Or they might say, I can feel the cold fingers of death tugging on me. It's something the mortals use to say as they lay dying."

"Well, yes, but what does that have to do with you?"

"When I get too close, the mortals feel that chill, and it scares them because they don't know what it is. If they are on their deathbed, the mortal understands why they feel it. It's because their death is close at hand. Those that are healthy and flush with life, not so much."

"I have never felt a chill around you."

"That is because you are a god, immortal," Thanatos intoned.

"Oh."

"I have always blamed my size or the expression on my face. Sometimes I even blame my attitude for mortals shying from me, but it's all a lie. It's a lie I tell myself to make me feel better, but it rarely works. Anyway, mortals turn from me because I am the personification of death, and they feel it even though they don't understand it. That is also why I wish to hold on to my sweet Andrina. She doesn't feel that coldness. She doesn't fear me. When she sees me, she sees the man in me, not the god of death, and I like that," Thanatos finished in Greek. Then, without another word, he walked away, leaving Apollo staring after him.

CHAPTER TWELVE

"Good morning, Andrina," Kristos said as Andrina walked into the kitchen.

Andrina returned his greeting with a soft "good morning" of her own as she grabbed a bowl to make herself some cereal.

"So, I saw Mom go into your room this morning," Kristos began after taking a sip of coffee.

Andrina could feel his eyes shrewdly watching her as she sat down. Not saying anything, just giving him a nod, she sat down and began to eat. She honestly didn't want to get into it with her brother because arguing with her mother earlier had been enough drama for one morning.

Kristos huffed, showing her how irritated he was. He then reached across the table and took her hand, waiting for her to glance up. When she finally did, he softly said, "I told you I'd give him a chance, Andrina, and I stand by my word. Now, tell me what Mom said. You seem upset, and I don't like seeing you upset."

Andrina put her spoon down and whispered, "She thinks he's strange and believes he's hiding things from me. Because of that, she doesn't want me to continue seeing him."

"Hm... well, you said yourself that he has secrets," Kristos murmured back.

"They aren't dangerous secrets though. Besides, everyone has secrets we keep and only tell the special people in our lives."

"Okay, I get the secret thing. I have things I wouldn't tell just anyone, either. Also, you did mention how Crusher told them to you."

She nodded and smiled at Kristos, thankful he seemed to understand.

"Which is a good thing because it means he isn't hiding stuff, at least not from you, and is trying to start this relationship right. As much as I hate to admit it, I don't need to know his secrets because I'm not the one dating him." Kristos chuckled when she crossed her eyes at him. "Let it be known, I still don't like him, but I'll try and be polite for your sake. Also, I reserve the right to go all big brother on him sometimes just to keep him in line."

"I would expect no less from you, Kristos, and I

love you for it because I know it's because you care," Andrina whispered as she blinked back her tears. She knew he was trying to treat her as a brother should and watch out for her, even if it sometimes annoyed her. "Thanks, Kristos. It means a lot to me that you are willing to put your feelings about him aside and let me have this."

Kristos squeezed her hand before pulling back and picking up his coffee. "I wouldn't worry too much; Mom will come around."

"She did promise not to stand in my way by the end of our conversation." Then, with a slight flush on her cheeks, she admitted, "I sincerely hope you're right, and she does come around because I love him, Kristos, I honestly do."

Kristos raised his eyebrows as he asked, "Love? Are you sure what you feel for him at this point is love?"

"That's pretty much what I said," Mom said as she walked in. Making her way to the counter, she grabbed a coffee cup and filled it.

"I'll tell Kristos, just like I told you, Mom, I love him with every beat of my heart," Andrina said, picking her spoon back up. "I hope to marry him, have his cute babies, and grow old and gray with him."

"You did not say all that to me, Andrina," Mom said in an annoyed tone as she sat down at the table.

"Well, I'm telling you now," Andrina declared. "Oh, and Kristos, I invited him to our birthday party."

"Okay," Kristos said with a disgruntled sigh. Picking up his coffee cup once more, he stated, "I don't see someone with the name Skull Crusher as being the party type. Are you sure he'll be comfortable there around all our friends?"

Andrina sighed as she pushed her now empty bowl away. She answered him, saying, "No. Crusher told me it would be awkward for him because he does tend to make people nervous."

"That he does," Mom muttered.

Andrina glanced at her mom to see she was now glowering down into her coffee cup as if her coffee had the answer to her life issues. "I know he makes you nervous, Mom. So, I won't bring him around here much, but it won't keep me from seeing him. He's a wonderful man despite what anyone else thinks, and he makes me happy. That's what truly matters, isn't it?"

Mom gave Andrina a slight smile as she answered, "Yes, that is what matters the most. Andrina, you are my child, and I only want what is best for you and your brother. If this Crusher fellow is what you think is best for you, then I'll be behind you all the way, but I still feel it was too quick. So, all I'm asking is that you be careful because I don't want to see you hurt."

Andrina stood and walked around to the back of her mom's chair. Leaning over, she wrapped her arms around her shoulders and lay her cheek against her mom's. "He won't hurt me. Yes, it may seem as if everything is moving too fast, but deep inside, I know he's the only man for me." Pulling away, she straightened and walked to the counter. She then poured herself a cup of coffee and sat back down. "So, where is the party going to be held this year?"

A big smile crossed her mom's face as she twisted in her seat to face Andrina.

Her mom loved to throw parties, and Andrina knew she tried to outdo herself every year.

Mom started by animatedly saying, "I was thinking…"

Andrina sat back, chuckling as Kristos gave a bored sigh, but he sat and listened anyway. He was such a good brother and son.

Focusing her attention back on her mom, she sighed happily. *I think this might be the first party I have enjoyed in a long time, all because Thanatos will be with me. So, let the party planning began.*

———

Thanatos pulled up into Andrina's driveway and had barely shut off his motorcycle when she came out the front door. She came bouncing down the steps and ran to where he was parked. She was pulling on the leather jacket she'd bought on their shopping trip the weekend before as she came to meet him.

He smiled at the memory of that shopping trip because it had been a joyous one. He usually hated being around so many mortals because of their reactions to him. Yet, as he'd gone from store to store with Andrina, she had made him forget everything but her laughter and smiles. It had indeed been a good day.

They'd been dating for a few weeks now, and Thanatos felt so blessed to have Andrina in his life because she had changed it for the better. He genuinely believed he loved her more with every day that went by. Andrina became his temptation the moment he had run into her. Now she was that and so much more.

"Thanatos!" Andrina excitedly exclaimed when she reached him. Leaning in close, she kissed him twice, in quick succession. "Tomorrow is my birthday party, but I'm glad you came to see me tonight too."

"Nothing could keep me away from you, my sweet temptation," Thanatos murmured to her in Greek. Reaching up, he cupped his hand around her neck to bring her in for another kiss. When he knew she needed air, he broke the kiss. Switching back to

English, he told her, "Everyone is going to be at Marlo's Diner for dinner. I thought now would be a good time to introduce you to the rest of the MC."

Andrina pulled back and gave him a grin before saying, "That sounds lovely."

"I'm not sure that lovely is the right word for it, but hop on, and we'll go anyway," Thanatos said as he patted the seat behind him.

Andrina poked her lip out slightly as she asked, "Another kiss first? Since we won't be alone for most of the evening, I need to feed my kissing addiction first."

Thanatos grinned and pulled her into his lap.

Andrina squealed as her feet left the ground, her arms coming up to wrap around his neck. She laughed as she exclaimed, "Thanatos!"

He didn't bother to answer; he just kissed her again. Many kisses later, he pulled away and put her back on her feet. "If we don't go now, we will be going to my house instead of to dinner. I know you want to wait to make love, but the wait is getting so much harder."

Andrina sighed as she put on the helmet he now held out to her. In a whisper, she agreed, "I know. Let's just get through the party, and then we'll talk again. I promise."

Thanatos nodded and waited for her to climb on behind him before starting his motorcycle up. Once she had her arms wrapped tightly around him, he took off down the driveway. Within minutes they were pulling up in the parking lot of Marlo's Diner and parking. Glancing around and counting the motorcycles, he realized they were the last to show up. He helped Andrina off, took the helmet when she handed it to him and placed it in his saddlebag. Holding out his hand, Thanatos waited for Andrina to take hold before leading her toward the diner door.

"I hope everyone likes me," Andrina told him when they reached the door.

Thanatos paused in reaching for the door handle and glanced at her. "They are gods and goddesses. Most of them rarely like anyone. So, please try not to take it personally."

Andrina gave a heavy sigh as she told him, "Okay, I'll try not to. Maybe Irina and Cathy will like me, at least I hope they will."

Thanatos grinned as he informed her, "They, I have no doubt, will love you."

He opened the door, his hand on her lower back, and encouraged her to enter. Walking inside, they headed for the back, where everyone was already seated. He felt as if everyone in the establishment was holding their breath as he walked by and felt like growling. It was times like this he wished Zeus would just rent the place out for the evening so that he wouldn't have to deal with the mortals being there to eat.

"Wow, rude much?" Andrina asked in a soft tone. "I don't think I've had people stare at me as much in my life as they have in the five minutes we've been here. Although, some of them are trying to do it inconspicuously."

"It isn't you, darling. They are staring at me," Thanatos told her. "Remember the chill? They feel it as I pass, catching their attention; you just happen to be with me."

"Oh, so being weirded out gives them a right to stare and be rude?" Andrina asked as she glanced up at him. She answered her own question by saying, "No, no, it does not. No matter how you feel, it is impolite to stare."

By that time, they were at the table full of the MC, and Thanatos heard Eros snicker before he mentioned, "I like her already. She is correct. Rude is rude no matter how much you pretty it up."

Andrina turned to focus on Eros as she nodded and said, "I know, right?" Then as she held out her hand to shake, she told him, "I'm Andrina."

"I'm Crossbow," Eros told her as he took her hand. However, instead of shaking, he kissed the back of it.

Andrina giggled and said, "Well, aren't you sweet."

"I am, yet you're with him," Eros stated. Poking his lower lip poked out, he faked a pout as he pointed at Thanatos.

Thanatos bared his teeth in a silent snarl as he glowered at Eros.

Andrina wrapped her arms around Thanatos' waist and leaned into him. She was not taken in at all by the twinkle of mischief in Eros's eye. She belonged to one man and was proud enough of it to declare, "Yes, and happily so."

Thanatos relaxed in her arms; she tilted her head up to smile at him. He winked, and she laughed softly.

Eros cleared his throat, bringing their attention back to him. He continued with, "This is Prophet next to me and his sister Claws. Although, I believe you've already met Prophet."

"I have," Andrina agreed as she nodded her head. Glancing over at Prophet, she saw he was glaring at her and was slightly taken aback by it. *What did I ever do to him?* Having no idea what the answer was, she quickly turned her attention back to the introductions.

"We then have Mad Dog and his ol' lady Cathy;

Doom and his ol' lady Irina, and last of the couples is Tank and his wife, Queen," Eros said.

Thanatos leaned in and whispered, "Apollo, and Artemis, Ares, Hades, Zeus, and Hera."

Andrina's eyes widened as she stared at the last couple mentioned. Zeus smirked, and Hera thumbed her nose in the air. In a whisper, she asked, "Why did he introduce Hera as Zeus's wife instead of his ol' lady?"

"Because Hera would rip Eros a new one if he dared to call her old in any fashion."

"Oh, yeah..." Andrina murmured.

"Next is Vixen, Ambush, Shark, and last is Brewer," Eros said, finishing the introductions.

"That would be Aphrodite, Athena, Poseidon, and Dionysus," Thanatos informed Andrina softly.

"Maybe the two of you should sit down now so that we can all order," Zeus suggested in a demanding tone. "We had to wait on you to get here, don't make us wait longer so you can chit chat. I'm hungry."

Thanatos raised his eyebrows at the comment as he pulled out a chair for Andrina to sit. *Since when does Zeus wait for anyone?*

"I apologize for making you wait," Andrina politely said as she let her gaze move around the table. "I had to work late, so Crusher came a bit later to pick me up than was originally planned."

"We don't need your excuses, girl," Hera said snidely, "What we need is for you to sit down as Zeus told you to do."

Andrina gasp and Thanatos glared at Hera. He didn't say anything because he knew it would only cause more problems. Instead, he squeezed Andrina's hand and kissed the side of her head as he murmured, "Ignore them, darling."

Andrina nodded and turned her attention to the waitress who was now standing at Zeus's side.

With a smile, the waitress began taking orders. Once the orders were complete, she left but quickly returned with the drinks and handed them out, leaving once more.

When she left the second time, Zeus turned his attention once more to Andrina. "So, girl, what do you do, or are you still in school? You look young."

Andrina nervously licked her lips as she stared at the god, Zeus. She then politely murmured, "No, I'm not still in school, though I suppose I am still young since I'm only twenty-three. As far as what I do, I work part-time in a little boutique. I paint and sculpt in my free time."

"Ah, so you think of yourself as an artist?" Apollo asked.

Andrina shrugged as she watched the waitress slowly deliver the food around the table. Finally, she answered, "I would like to be, but I fear I'm not as good at it as I could be. I do understand that you are quite a painter."

Apollo gave a slight nod, the glare leaving his face as he sighed, "I suppose Skull told you that?"

"He did, and he told me it is only one of your many talents," Andrina agreed. "Perhaps you could teach me a thing or two?"

Thanatos spoke up, a growl in his tone as he answered for Apollo, saying, "No, no, he cannot."

Andrina glanced over at her love, shocked at the glare of anger on his face. "Why ever not? He's an artist, which is what I'd like to be, and he could help me accomplish that goal."

A laugh from Aphrodite had Andrina's gaze swinging her way. Aphrodite laughed again before informing her, "You truly don't see it, do you, girl?"

"See what exactly?" Andrina questioned, feeling confused.

"Skull is quite possessive of you, dear," Aphrodite answered. "I've only seen the two of you together for ten minutes, and yet I see it on his face and in his actions.

Andrina turned her attention back to Thanatos, who did have a dark look on his face. Thanatos had pulled his eyebrows together over eyes which flickered in and out with red flames.

"He doesn't wish for you to become enamored with Prophet," Aphrodite continued. "We all know that Prophet is quite the ladies' man. Surely you know that as well."

Andrina sighed in annoyance at how silly Thanatos was as she continued to take in his tight jaw and downturned lips. *Thanatos knows that I love him. It seems to me he should have no doubts by now. So, what is going on between him and Apollo?*

"Andrina," Eros said softly, catching her attention. He leaned closer to her and whispered, "Skull, and most everyone else, call Prophet 'golden boy' for a reason. Prophet can do no wrong in the eyes of Zeus, and most of the rest of us can do no right. He also has the look women adore…"

"The look?" Andrina softly asked.

"Blond hair, blue eyes."

"Oh, that," she said with an understanding nod. "The look of the boy next door. Just so you know, I'd rather have the tall, dark, and handsome any day."

"And in Skull, you have that in spades. Regardless, put the two of them side by side, and Prophet will be chosen ten times out of ten over Skull. Now, even though he knows of your love, it can't completely erase years of insecurities in such a short time. Give him time, continue to show him how much you love him, and, eventually, you will break through to him."

Andrina gave Eros a slight smile as he sat back in his chair. Returning her gaze to Thanatos, she found him glaring at the tabletop. Next, she realized the waitress was standing to the left of Thanatos, seemingly frozen in place. The girl seemed to be fearful of coming any closer so she could place their food in front of them.

Feeling unnaturally irritated, Andrina stood and grabbed the plates from the waitress. "Just go! If you can't do your job, then I'll do it for you." After placing the dishes on the table, she sat down. Leaning sideways, so she was right next to Thanatos' ear, not wanting anyone to hear, she whispered, "I love you, you big lug. However, if you don't stop trying to glare a hole in the table, which has done nothing to you, I'll be forced to come up with a way to punish you for it later."

Thanatos' head came up, and he stared at her. His eyes were wide; his mouth opens slightly in his shock.

Andrina snickered and leaned in to push his chin up, closing his mouth. After she gave him a chaste kiss, she said, "Now that I have your attention, let's eat because I'm starving."

"Another one has unquestionably bitten the dust," Apollo grumbled before shoving a fork full of food into his mouth.

Hearing him and knowing he meant for her to,

Andrina smirked. Glancing over to where he sat across from her, she agreed, "Yes, and I can't wait for it to be your turn."

Apollo snorted but said nothing else. Instead, he turned to talk to his sister and ignored Andrina.

With a shrug, she picked up her fork. Conversation with Apollo wasn't on her to-do list anyway. Nope, eating was, and so that is what she began to do.

CHAPTER THIRTEEN

Two hours later, Thanatos pulled up in Andrina's driveway and shut his motorcycle off.

Andrina climbed off from behind him only to straddle the seat in front of him.

"Darling, what are you doing?"

"I want some more kisses before I have to say goodnight," Andrina replied as she cupped his cheeks in her hands.

Wrapping his own hands around her waist, he held her gently. "Mm… I'd like that too. First, though, I'd like to ask you something. Did you have a good time?"

"I did, although I could have done without Hera's obnoxious comments," she answered. "Other than that, most everyone was polite enough."

Thanatos nodded. Giving in to the temptation of her pink lips, he leaned in to kiss her. Her head tilted, encouraging him to deepen the kiss as his hands began to search for a way under her shirt. Finally feeling bare skin, he groaned at the soft silkiness of it. He pulled her closer, his arousal now seated at the juncture of her thighs.

Oh, how I want her. I want her in my life, and my bed, for all time. I can't, won't let her walk away from me, not now, not ever. Andrina is mine.

Pulling away from her, he continued his kisses along her jaw until he reached her ear. After nibbling lightly on the lobe, he murmured, "Come home with me, darling. Say you will be mine now."

Andrina moaned, her eyes fluttering closed. "We were going to wait…" she whimpered, her head tilting to give him more room to place kisses on her neck, "until after my party. Remember? Then I'll be all yours, and you'll be mine, always and forever."

"I can't wait any longer for you to be one with me, *glyké mou peirasmé.* I need you to be by my side now," Thanatos enlightened her. He then forced himself to pull away from her, desperately seeking his self-control as he gazed at her beauty.

Andrina's eyes slowly fluttered open and locked with his. She brought her hand up and cupped his jaw, gently caressing it as her gaze held his. *My sweet temptation is what Thanatos just called me in Greek. He doesn't realize, at least not yet, how much of a temptation he is to me.*

"It's only one more day and barely that considering it is almost midnight now. I believe you will survive a few more hours, no matter how much you tempt me to be naughty with you."

Thanatos breathed in deeply, his eyes dark with his desire.

Andrina could see he was struggling with his wants and his promise. It was a fact that most of the gods got what they wanted from mortals; they used everything in their godly arsenal to make sure of it. Regardless, he had made her a promise, and she knew he would do his best to keep it.

"I promise only to sleep, nothing else," Thanatos implored as he gave her his best hangdog expression.

Andrina laughed and rubbed her nose against his before standing up. "Make all the promises you want, my love, but we want each other too much to behave. If I go home with you, we both know that sleeping is not what we would be doing because I can't keep my hands off you any more than you can keep yours off me."

Thanatos hummed softly but nodded as he agreed, "You're right."

"Of course, I am," Andrina said. "You know I want us to be married before that happens."

"I know."

Andrina sobered up as a thought crossed her mind, and she asked, "Tell me something, Thanatos, will you tire of me when I no longer carry the beauty of youth?"

Thanatos pulled her back into his lap as he told her, "Darling, I plan to make you mine in every way I can. You will be my friend, my lover, my wife, and I will be a friend, lover, and husband to you. However, to become those three things for me, you must also become as I am. Once I take you as my wife, I will not give you up to age or mortal death."

Andrina stared into his eyes as she asked, "How?"

"I am capable of giving you immortality, just as Hades and Ares did for their brides," he answered. "Did you honestly think I would have let it go this far if I didn't have a plan?"

"I didn't know," Andrina whispered. "I love you, Thanatos, and I would love to be your friend, your lover, your bride. I would also love to be the mother of your children someday."

Thanatos leaned in with a groan to kiss her. He was breathless, as was she when he pulled back and stated, "You need to go in now, for if you do not, I will not be letting you go tonight."

Andrina took in a deep breath as she stood up. "Good night, Thanatos. I will see you tomorrow night."

"Do you want me to come and pick you up or just meet you at the party?"

"I think it best if you meet me there," she informed him. "If you were to come and pick me up, I might just have you drive us far away from here instead of to the hotel."

"Oh, and where would we go?"

"Somewhere we could get married, of course."

"Where might that be?"

Quickly thinking, Andrina remembered hearing how you could run off to Las Vegas to one of their chapels. "Vegas? Although, I think you still have to have a marriage license if you want it to be legal."

Thanatos chuckled, "I can arrange that very easily. I could have us there in the time it would take you to blink, and I could probably get a license almost as fast with the help of Eros."

"I know. So, I think it would be best if we don't tempt ourselves."

"You will always be *peirasmé mou,* that will never change," Thanatos said.

The words, *my temptation,* echoed in her head, making her blood heat with the need to throw her cares to the wind and ride away with him tonight.

Inwardly fanning herself, she took a calming breath and admitted, "I know, and it makes me all warm and happy, inside and out."

Thanatos smiled, happiness pounding inside him like a bass drum with every beat of his heart. He was so close to making her his, and he couldn't screw this up. He took a calming breath to keep from pulling her back to him and asked, "Where is the party taking place? I have forgotten."

"The ballroom of the Statesman Hotel. You know where it is?"

"*Nai,*" Thanatos agreed with a nod. "I'll be there."

Andrina blew him a kiss and began to walk up the stairs to her house.

Thanatos watched her until she'd entered the house and was no longer in his sight. He then started his motorcycle and roared off down the street. It was going to be a long night, and he knew there would be little sleep for him.

"One more night, *peirasmé mou,* then you will be mine because I have waited long enough," he promised. "Even if I have to get Eros to marry us without your family there, you will be in my bed tomorrow night."

Satisfied with his plan, he headed for his favorite lookout spot to while away the rest of the night. When he got there, he sat back in his stone chair and breathed deeply of the night air. The lights of the city twinkled in front of him, and somehow it gave him peace.

"I'm guessing this is where you like to hide out when you should be busy pretending to work."

Thanatos groaned silently at being bothered but glanced over at Eros just the same. "So, what if it is?"

Eros walked closer and stood next to him, gazing out at the town also. "It is a lovely view. I believe you could see the whole town if it were daylight."

"Perhaps, but that isn't why I come here. Now, are you going to tell me why *you're* here?"

Eros chuckled as he snapped his fingers. A sturdy outdoor chair appeared, and he sat down in it.

"Yes, pull up a chair and have a seat," Thanatos grumbled. "Act as if I invited you to come and stay awhile."

"Don't mind if I do." Eros stretched out his legs and folded his arms over his chest. He sat silent, not saying a word and the silence seemed to stretch into hours.

Finally, exasperated with the other god, Thanatos growled, "Well?"

"I thought perhaps you might have something to

ask me by now," Eros answered, turning his head to gaze at Thanatos fully. "Or perhaps not."

Thanatos stared at Eros, whose eyes seemed to be full of amusement at his expense. Thinking hard, he tried to figure out what the god was speaking about but honestly had no clue.

Eros wiggled his eyebrows and began to whistle a tune.

The tune sounded vaguely familiar. Thanatos knew he'd heard it somewhere before, but where?

"Oh, why do I bother with you, Neanderthals? None of you have a lick of romance in you, but I keep hoping," Eros grumbled. "I'm sure Andrina would have known what I was whistling."

"Maybe your whistling skills are bad."

"They are not!" Eros exclaimed. "My skills are perfect, so it must mean your ears are the problem."

Thanatos snorted in disbelieve. "Fine, want to clue me in since I don't have a clue what your song was supposed to be."

"It was 'Here Comes the Bride,'" Eros informed him, sounding haughty. "I thought by now you would have the girl ready to say, 'I do' in a crowd full of family and friends."

Thanatos grinned as he leaned back and stared down at the city once more. "Andrina is ready. We're just waiting to get her birthday party out of the way."

"Ooh! Parties, I love a good party," Eros informed Thanatos with a big grin. "I might have to show up, incognito, of course, and dance with a few pretty girls."

Thanatos barely resisted the urge to roll his eyes at the god of love. "Just be ready to marry Andrina and me when the time comes."

"Trust me, I will be more than ready," Eros informed him. Then, with a snap of his fingers, he and his chair disappeared in a cloud of red smoke.

Thanatos closed his eyes and breathed deeply of the fresh air once more. Alone again, his thoughts returned to his beautiful bride-to-be. A grin slowly spread over his face. *Yes, life is good and will only get better once Andrina is mine.*

Andrina slipped quietly into the house and closed the door. Taking a deep breath, she began to make her way to the stairs, only to be stopped by a throat clearing behind her. Turning one hand on the banister to steady her, she glanced behind her.

Kristos was leaning on the door jamb of the sitting room, arms crossed, watching her.

"So, you finally decided to come inside," Kristos commented as he straightened and shoved his hands into his pockets. "I was beginning to wonder if you planned to spend the whole night out in the driveway kissing Crusher."

Andrina felt her face heat up at the thought of her brother spying on her and Thanatos. In a curt tone, she asked, "Why were you spying on us, Kristos?"

"Just making sure you were all right," Kristos informed her. "Andrina, you are my sister, and all I want is to see you happy."

"Crusher makes me happy," she reminded him again.

Kristos huffed. "I know. You've told me multiple times, but sometimes hearing it and seeing it are two different things. So, I wanted to see for myself that what you were telling me was true."

"Oh, so now you're calling me a liar?" Andrina asked, feeling anger fill her.

Kristos shook his head as he said, "No, that is not what I'm saying at all. I know you don't want to hear this, Andrina, but I really do have your best interest at heart, and sometimes I might not do things exactly the way you want, but I do it for you. You are my sister, and I love you."

Andrina sighed as she left the stairs and walked over to her brother. Stopping in front of him, she wrapped her arms around him, hugging him as she breathed in the scent of his favorite cologne.

Kristos wrapped his arms around her, holding her tight as he sighed into her hair, blowing it slightly.

"I know you do; I love you too." Loosening her grip on him, she tilted her head back so she could see his face as she demanded, "Now tell me exactly what you have been doing to prove to yourself that what I've told you is the truth."

"What makes you think I've been doing anything except for what I did tonight?"

Andrina laughed but still managed to narrow her eyes at him. "Because I know you, Kristos. Spill it!"

Kristos huffed and pulled her back to him, resting his chin once more on the top of her head. He admitted, "Okay, so, I guess I have been a little stalkerish of late. I followed the two of you a couple of times because I wanted to see how he treated you when the two of you were alone."

"Oh?"

"Yeah, and I honestly liked what I saw," Kristos confessed, though he sounded reluctant to do so.

"Tell me then, what did you see?"

"I saw a man who opened doors, pulled out chairs, held your hand, a man who protected you," Kristos began. "I saw a man who smiled at you even as he glowered at the rest of the world. I saw the man who gazes at you as if the sun rises with your smile and sets in your eyes. I saw a man who is totally and completely in love with my sister, and I liked what I saw because I know he will give you everything he has to give and more. I saw a man I believe is worthy of my sister. I also saw a woman who stared at that big ugly biker the same way and realized she feels the same way about him."

"Oh, Kristos," Andrina cried. Tears began to well up in her eyes and spill over as she pulled back to connect their eyes again. "I do love Crusher. With everything in me, I love that man. He may be big, and to you, he may be nothing but a rough and tough man in a motorcycle club. To me, he is my love and my very heart. I can no longer imagine my world without him, and I'm going to marry him just as soon as possible." She laughed and added, "I honestly think he would have already married me, but I told him he had to wait until after our party tomorrow."

Kristos sighed and informed her, "Andrina, just because I accept him doesn't mean Mom will. She doesn't like how nervous he makes her feel. She says it's unnatural."

Andrina sighed as she lay her head on his chest once more. She knew precisely why Thanatos made her mom nervous, but it wasn't her secret to tell. So, she replied, "I know, but I am going to marry him, and I won't let her stop me. Yes, he's different, maybe even strange somehow, but my love for him doesn't see that. All I see is a man, a man with a big heart. Crusher is a man who deserves to be loved as much as I do, Kristos. I also see a man who wants me to be happy and plans to do everything he can to make sure it happens. That's what I see when I gaze at Crusher."

"If that is what you see, then I will try and see it too."

Andrina jerked away from her brother, turning to stare at her mother. Her mom was standing at the foot of the stairs, tears streaming down her face.

"Mom? Did you hear…" Andrina began, only to taper off at her mother's nod.

"I did hear the whole conversation. Oh, Andrina, I love you, and I only wish for you to be happy," Mom told Andrina as she stepped off the stairs. Moving over to where Andrina stood, she pulled her into a hug. "If he truly makes you happy, then I won't stand in your way any longer."

"Thanks, Mom, thank you so much," Andrina cried as she hugged her mom tightly.

"Now, tomorrow is going to be a long day," Mom murmured as she stepped back, wiping her tears. "I would suggest we all get some rest."

Thanatos heaved a heavy sigh as he moved about his home in the Underworld. He had to admit; he was a bit nervous about the party he was going to in less than an hour.

"All those people. What was I thinking, telling her I'd go?"

"Yes, what were you thinking?"

Thanatos turned to find Hades and Irina standing behind him.

Hades looked grumpy with a sour expression on his face. Irina, however, had a happy smile on her face.

Thanatos figured it must have been the little lady's idea to visit him. So, giving a slight bow, he sarcastically asked, "To what do I owe the pleasure of your company, King Hades?"

Irina snickered.

Hades grumbled under his breath before saying, "It wasn't my idea to come; I'm sure you figured that out already. Irina, however, seems to think we can help you with your problem."

Thanatos crossed his arms, widened his stance, and flexed his wings. "What problem would that be?"

"I believe Andrina said she invited you to her birthday party," Irina answered.

Thanatos nodded as he answered, "*Nai.*"

"Big guy like you doesn't strike me as being the partying type," Irina continued.

"That would be a correct assumption," Thanatos readily agreed.

Irina went on, "So, I thought perhaps if you didn't have to go alone…"

"Ah, Irina, thank you for the thought, but I'm not sure it would be the best of ideas for a bunch of bikers to show up at a fancy party," Thanatos murmured uneasily. "It's being held in the ballroom of the Statesmen Hotel, which I understand is about as high class as you can get around here."

"Who said anything about a bunch of bikers showing up?" Irina asked indignantly. "I just meant that Hades and I could go with you. I also thought that you and he could dress like the rich men you are instead of like penniless bikers."

Hades snorted at his wife, and to Thanatos, it seemed as if he was trying not to laugh.

Irina poked her lip out at Hades before she added, "What Zeus doesn't know about, he can't yell about, and I won't tell on you."

Thanatos couldn't help but snicker at her Zeus comment. She was right though; if Zeus knew about her plan, he'd yell, long and loud. Zeus wanted them all to stay in character, and to stray from his strict edicts was not acceptable.

"I believe it's time those snobby people saw what a wonderful person Andrina is and that she has a wonderful man to boot," Irina finished, her face flushed with excitement.

Thanatos stared at the woman, wondering if she'd lost her mind. Zeus' anger aside, going to this party was still a bad idea. Surely, she realized how uncomfortable the mortals would be in his company; after all, she was mortal.

Unless she one of the few mortals who, strangely, doesn't feel the chill that comes off me in waves. Then, feeling slightly dense, he remembered something. Thanks to Hades, Irina was now immortal. Which meant she wouldn't feel the chill coming from him. He sighed. *Irina won't understand unless I explain it to her or at least try to.*

CHAPTER FOURTEEN

Taking a deep breath, Thanatos asked, "Irina, have you ever felt a chill go through you for no reason at all? Did it make you glance around, puzzled, as you stood shivering and wondering what had happened?"

Irina frowned, glancing at Hades.

Hades shrugged. "What can I say except, I am a god. I do not feel hot or cold as mortals do."

Returning her gaze to Thanatos, Irina answered, "I suppose I probably have, but I can't say it's something I remember. Sorry."

"Perhaps you were in the room when someone died at some point in your life?" Thanatos continued.

Irina slowly blinked, her face blank. Then as if she'd finally fit the puzzle pieces together, she slowly nodded. "Oh, I remember now; I was in the hospital room when my grandmother passed. I was only eight or nine at the time, but I vaguely remember a strange cold filling the room just after Mom said Grandmother was gone. It only lasted a moment, though, and at that age didn't make much of an impression on me. So, I never really thought about it afterward."

"That was me," Thanatos told her.

"What?" Irina asked.

"That was me, you felt. At that moment, Death was in the room. I was in the room, coming to take her spirit," Thanatos explained. "Coldness is all a mortal feels when I'm around, but they don't see me. Although sometimes the one dying catch just a glimpse of me right before I prepare to take their spirit away with me."

"Huh, I didn't know," Irina said, her head tilted thoughtfully.

"Most don't, or they prefer not to think about it either way," Thanatos said. "Now, think about that cold chill rushing over your body, never leaving, staying, and turning your body to ice as it tries to fight the unknown chill. That is what those people at that party will feel if I stand close to them for more than a moment or two."

"You mean they will feel the cold of death even though you aren't there to take a spirit?" Irina asked. "Seriously?"

"Seriously, they will," Thanatos agreed. "You don't

feel the chill now, of course, since you are no longer mortal. However, those at the party will feel it, and it will make them uncomfortable to be around me."

"So, this isn't about whether you like parties after all," Irina huffed with a slight laugh.

"If only it were that simple," Thanatos stated. "I genuinely don't feel comfortable going to parties. It's true. But no, disliking them isn't the reason for my hesitation to go. Regardless, I would do anything for *glyké mou peirasmé*, so I will go. If you would like to go for moral support, Irina, I'm sure Andrina wouldn't mind the company of someone with whom she could converse. Just know, we don't plan to stay any longer than we have to."

Thanatos watched as Irina turned her focus on Hades, her brow wrinkled up in a frown.

Seemingly Hades knew what she wanted to know and answered, "He said, 'my sweet temptation.'"

"Ah," Irina quietly said before she turned back to Thanatos with a smile. "That is so sweet of you to do that for her. You talk as if no one will talk to her, though. Does she not have any friends at all?"

"She does. Only a few though who are close and personal."

"Is there going to be someone there that will give her a hard time?" Irina asked him next.

"Most of those who will be there are her brother's

friends. From what Andrina has told me, he is immensely popular," Thanatos explained. He then took a deep breath and let it out slowly. "Also, according to Andrina, most of her brother's friends don't like her for one reason or another."

"I'm guessing they don't treat her the best," Irina softly said, her mouth drooping in a frown.

"They do not," Thanatos agreed, curling his lip up in a silent snarl. He hated the idea of his woman being mistreated by anyone. "When he isn't around, they are quite vicious, from what I understand."

"Does he know how they treat her?" Irina inquired.

"*Óchi*. Andrina has not told him because she doesn't want him to kick them out of his life," Thanatos stated. "She refuses to be the reason Kristos discards those he calls his friends."

"Oh, that is so sad," Irina murmured with a frown. Suddenly though, she smiled. "She'll get to know us, Thanatos, and we'll be her friends. Cathy, her and me, we'll have great times together and she'll forget all about those horrible people."

Thanatos nodded, not knowing exactly what to say. As much as he hoped they would get along he wouldn't comment Andrina to anything without her first giving her consent. So, Irina would just have to take it up with Andrina when she saw her. He wasn't digging himself a hole he couldn't get out of by putting in his two cents worth in.

"We should go now and get ready," Irina suggested. "Shall we take a limo?"

Thanatos chuckled at the sudden change of subject, but answered, "I believe Andrina would be disappointed if I didn't drive my motorcycle."

"I don't claim to know much about women's fashion, Thanatos. However, I saw what Irina was thinking of wearing if we were to go with you. I don't think it would be appropriate for the back of my bike," Hades said.

"Short, tight dresses would make it hard to straddle the seat, and might show more skin than she wants to," Irina mentioned. "A long dress could be dangerous to wear since it could get caught in a tire or something."

Thanatos frowned, realizing he had no idea what Andrina planned to wear. So, taking out his phone, he began type out a text, deciding it was best to ask here rather than assume. "Perhaps I should find out what she plans to wear."

"Perhaps you should, then let us know," Irina suggested with a laugh. Then she and Hades disappeared in a haze of black smoke.

Thanatos' phone rang, a glance told him it was Andrina. Swiping his finger across the answer button, he said, "Hello, darling. Tell me, what will you be wearing tonight?"

On the other end of the phone, Andrina laughed as she imparted, "A fancy long dress, of course, and my brother will be wearing a tux. I thought I told you this the day after you agreed to come, didn't I?"

"You may have, but it seems to have slipped my mind. I needed to know because Hades and Irina wish to come with me, and Irina suggested we take a limo."

"Oh, that would be a nice way for you to arrive. You will have all the women swooning when you step out of it all duded up in a tux."

"You are the only woman I wish to have swoon with one glance at my face," Thanatos said with a bit of a growl to his voice.

Andrina chuckled. "I know, my love, and I probably will swoon when I see you. You do realize how the three of you arrive doesn't really matter since I won't be with you, we agreed to meet there."

"I know, but Irina wants a limo, so I suppose I'll agree to it."

"Good, the lady deserves to ride in style," Andrina said. "We have money, but barely rent a limo for anything. I've enjoyed them the few times I've ridden in one though."

"You were dropped off by one the day you visited me at the shop," Thanatos reminded her.

"True, I did," Andrina agreed. "I mostly did that just to spite Kristos, I had the bill sent to him since he hid my car keys."

Thanatos chuckled at her deviousness.

"I was thinking we would leave the party alone," Andrina mentioned to him. "Which means there would be no need for such extravagances as far as I'm concerned."

"Oh, don't you worry, darling, I plan for us to leave alone limo or not. Fair warning, I have plans for the birthday girl," Thanatos told her.

Andrina hummed softly on the other end of the line but said nothing.

"However, Hades will have no problem affording the extravagance and I'm sure he and Irina will enjoy going home in it alone later."

"I'll just bet you're right," Andrina murmured. She then giggled softly before adding, "I know Hades seems gruff, but I have a feeling he won't have problems being all kinds of naughty when he gets her alone in that car."

"You would be right," Thanatos said gruffly. Now he was thinking about how he'd like to skip the party altogether and be naughty with Andrina. Time to let her go or he'd be going to her room and taking her away, then neither of them would be going. Clearing his throat, he said, "I'll let you go now, and I'll see you in less than an hour. I love you."

"I love you too," Andrina murmured before she hung up.

Thanatos instantly sent Hades a text and they made plans on where to meet and a time.

Feeling a bit more relaxed now that he wasn't going to be showing up by himself, he retracted his wings. Then he dressed in an all-black tux with a gray rosebud boutonniere on his lapel. With one last glance in the mirror, he left his home in the Underworld to meet up with Hades and Irina.

"Well, this is it, the Statesman Hotel," Irina murmured, from where she and Hades stood next to the limo.

Thanatos stepped out and stood next to them as the driver took off to find a parking place where he'd wait for their call. Staring up at the fancy hotel, he wished he could have just taken Andrina somewhere for a private celebration instead of going to this party.

"Come along Skull," Hades murmured, watchful of the mortals around them. "It's best not to keep a lady waiting."

"I know, but I seriously do not want to go in there," Thanatos admitted.

"For your lady, Skull," Irina encouraged. "You can do this for your lady. I have faith in you."

"For my lady," Thanatos repeated. "Andrina, my love, *peirasmé mou.*"

Straightening his jacket, Thanatos stepped forward and headed for the fancy double doors in a confident stride.

Hades and Irina stayed only a couple of steps to the left of him.

Standing next to the doors was an older gentleman wearing a black and navy uniform showing his position as the doorman. As the three of them drew close, the man opened the door, greeting them with, "Good evening, gentlemen, lady", and gave them a slight bow.

Thanatos moved as quickly through the doors as he could and still act mortal. Still, the doorman shivered slightly as he passed him. Although, the man did manage to keep a pleasant expression on his face despite the chill.

"Which way to the ballroom?" Hades asked gruffly as he paused just inside the door, Irina just ahead of him.

Thanatos stopped also, listening to the directions.

"Straight down the hall and to your left is a set of double doors. It's through there," the doorman answered. "I don't think I've seen you here before, but

I'm guessing you're here for the grand party that's going on."

"We are," Irina murmured her agreement clearly

"It's always a big to-do around here," the doorman told them with a big smile.

Thanatos could tell right then he was one of those mortals who would talk your ear off if you let them.

"Mrs. Dukakis is a nice lady and very well-liked. This is the fifth year I've been here for the party," the doorman continued as he rocked back slightly on his heels.

"Oh, and what do you think of her children?" Irina asked.

Thanatos almost smiled. Evidently, Irina saw the talkative man as a way to get more information.

The doorman laughed before he answered, "The girl is as sweet as she is pretty, the boy is polite and shows good manners. However, some of their friends? A snooty bunch, the whole lot of them. The maids hate to see them come because they always leave the worst messes. Most of them have more money than sense I believe, but it's only once a year, and the pay's good. So, we all do what we have to do."

"Thank you for the information, sir. Come on you two, we need to go now," Thanatos reminded them. He then set off down the hall, moving at a quick pace, impatient to see his woman now that he was here. If

Hades and Irina fell behind, so be it, they knew where he was headed.

"Hold up, hotshot," Irina called out from behind him. "This lady in a dress and high heel shoes is doing her best to walk and not break her ankle doing it. There is no way I'm running, so slow down!"

Thanatos paused at the double doors that would take them into the ballroom and took a minute to glance back. Behind him by a few feet, he could see Hades trying not to laugh as he gripped Irina's elbow. Irina was holding up her skirt off the floor with one hand, presumably to help her walk faster, wabbling as she went.

I do wonder what makes women wear shoes they find so hard to walk in. Give me a good comfortable pair of boots any day over those shoes with spikes on the heel. He shook his head in confusion but decided to politely wait for the couple to catch up with him. Once they were even with him, he turned toward the door and found yet another older gentleman stationed there.

The man gave them a dignified nod, though he was shaking slightly, and his lips were tinted blue. He quickly opened the door, his hand clenching as if he were about to shove the three of them through it.

He's probably hoping that once we're gone the strange cold which came on suddenly will leave just as quickly.

Thanatos felt like smacking himself for not paying

closer attention to his surroundings. He knew better than to stand that close to mortals and could have stood on the other side of the hall as he waited. He'd had other things on his mind though and hadn't even noticed the man was standing there. Sometimes he truly hated what he was, but it wasn't as if it could be changed.

Soon he would take his woman back to his home in the Underworld. Once there he would be able to relax and regroup from the stress of spending so much time in the mortal realm.

"Have a nice evening and enjoy the party," the doorman said as the three walked through the door.

The door slightly slammed behind them.

Irina jumped, letting out a quiet, "Oh," in surprise.

Hades chuckled and kissed her cheek before saying, "It was just the door, nothing to be scared of."

"I wasn't scared," Irina agued as she took everything in, her eyes open wide. "Well, this is interesting décor for a birthday party."

At her words, Thanatos began to glance around also. The ballroom was decked out in mostly white and gold decorations. There were gold balloons everywhere, floating close to the ceiling among the chandeliers. There were also large white columns that had golden flowerpots sitting on top of them, filled with white flowers of all kinds. Along the left wall, which was mostly windows, sheer white drapes had been hung. Across from it, on the right-hand wall, were life-sized statues.

Surely, those aren't statues of the gods, are they? Thanatos narrowed his eyes as he inspected the features and adornments on each of the statues. *Yes, I believe they are.*

Thanatos chuckled as he turned his head to focus on Hades who was now standing next to him. In Greek, he quietly asked, "Do you think you will find yourself among those statues?"

Hades shrugged and Irina grabbed his hand to tug him forward. Thanatos followed slowly behind the couple as they made their way over to where the statues stood.

Thanatos made sure he stayed slightly away from the crowd, he remembered the reaction of the doorman, which was gathered around to gaze at the statues. He watched as Hades swiveled his head from left to right. He knew exactly when Hades noticed the statue that was meant to be him because a frown settled on his face and his glare became even darker. If that were possible.

Thanatos knew Hades wouldn't have to walk any closer to realize it was indeed supposed to be a replica of him. Even he could tell just by the dog with three heads at the statue's feet. Other than that, its appearance was honestly nothing like Hades.

"Whose idea was this? Are they making a mockery of the gods?" Hades growled low in his throat, anger clearly showing on his face.

"Oh, now, honey, surely not," Irina soothed as she rubbed his arm gently. "Andrina is half Greek if you remember. I can't see her family making a mockery of them. Besides, how are they to know what the real Hades looks like? Or Cerberus, for that matter, since they've never seen him?"

"I suppose you're right," Hades muttered, still appearing irritated.

"Of course, I am," Irina said with a big grin. Then, in faltering Greek, she asked, "Did you find one of yourself, Thanatos?"

"No, I did not, but I think that might be Poseidon on the end. The statue is holding a trident and that appears to be waves at his feet," Thanatos murmured distractedly back in Greek as he turned away from them and the statues. They had lost his interest as his eyes roamed over the crowd, searching for Andrina.

Where is she, I need... wait, there she is. What is going on, why is she arguing with that girl? This is a party, there should be laughter, not anger. Best I go see what is going on, he decided.

Glancing over at Hades and Irina, he saw they were

now discussing another statue, which might have been Ares. Even as he began to walk away from them, he stated, "I have spotted Andrina."

"Lead the way," Hades muttered. He gave one last glare toward the statues before turning to follow.

CHAPTER FIFTEEN

"All right, Molly, I need you to bring out more of the caviar and cracker, maybe more spinach dip too since those items are going fast," Andrina told the worker. "Grab some of the fruit crepes also; they seemed low. When you return, make sure to take a quick peek at the drink table. With all the dancing, everyone is going to be thirsty."

"Yes, miss," Molly respectfully murmured before moving quickly toward the kitchen.

Andrina hummed, glancing once more at the tables covered in all kinds of hors d'oeuvres, wondering if any of the other foods needed replenishing. Usually, her mother took care of everything, but when she'd heard someone mention the hors d'oeuvres, she'd stopped the first server she'd seen.

Deciding there wasn't anything else, Andrina

began to glance around for Thanatos, hoping he would be there soon. Perhaps if she circled the room again, she'd spot him. Nodding to herself, she went to walk on, only to be jerked in a different direction than she'd planned.

"Oh!" Andrina exclaimed as someone began to pull her across the floor.

Andrina almost toppled over backward when she was brought to a quick halt, barely managing to catch herself against the wall. Straightening up with a huff, she glanced at the girl who had so rudely grabbed her and dragged her across the room. Running her hand over her hip, she tilted her head in confusion. "Excuse me, who do you think you are pulling me around like that?"

The girl snorted, her face showing disgust as she silently stared at Andrina.

"Since I'm pretty sure I don't know you, perhaps a better question would be, who are you?" Andrina asked as she took a moment to examine the girl. The girl was pretty, with her thick black hair in ringlets, pixie-like features, and wide blue eyes. She was slim and had a light tan that seemed natural with no lines showing on her shoulders, left bare by her strapless gown.

Andrina had to admit; the light peach floor-length gown flattered the girl's figure beautifully. However, the narrowed eyes and lips curled in disgust took away from that beauty and left her lacking in Andrina's eyes.

Finally, the girl spoke up, replying, "My name is Rachelle, and I'm your brother's fiancée."

Andrina gasp in shock, her jaw-dropping, which caused the girl to smirk. Shaking away the shock, and it was a shock because she and Kristos rarely kept secrets. The girl had to be out of her mind if she thought Kristos would keep something like this from her. "Fiancée? Kristos hasn't said anything about a girlfriend in months, much less a fiancée."

Rachelle gave a fake-sounding laugh that was high-pitched and had Andrina cringing at the sound. Running a hand through her hair, Rachelle preened as she said, "Well, I am his fiancée, or I will be when he proposes to me tonight. We've been dating for quite some time now.

"Seriously," Andrina murmured, not convinced. "Sounds to me like you jumped the gun on the proposal."

"Yes, seriously. Kristos will be proposing to me tonight; I feel it in my bones. Regardless, I'm genuinely not surprised he hasn't told you about me yet."

"Oh, and why is that?" Andrina asked, growing more puzzled by the moment. Glancing around, she hoped to spot Kristos. She needed to get away from this woman and find her brother and make him explain this mess to her.

"Because who would want to be around a dumpy little person such as yourself long enough to hold a conversation?" Rachelle asked. "The only reason I'm talking to you now is to tell you that you need to make yourself disappear. My friends and I don't like you, neither do Kristos's friends. Therefore, you don't need to be here."

"For your information, *Rachelle*, my brother and I tell each other everything. We always have…"

"Evidently, he doesn't, or you would have known he and I were dating," Rachelle interrupted her to say.

"Not only that," Andrina continued, ignoring Rachelle's accusation, "but I also don't think you have the right to kick me out of this party because it's my birthday just as much as it's Kristos's."

Rachelle grabbed hold of Andrina's arm. She dug her nails into the soft flesh until Andrina feared her arm would start to bleed. In a low voice, filled with venom, she sneered, "I don't care what you think. You, Andrina, are not wanted here tonight. Your brother only takes pity on you because his mom forces him to. So, don't think for one moment Kristos or anyone else will miss you if you leave."

Andrina felt tears well in her eyes, not only from the pain in her arm but from the words the girl had spoken. Her insecurities were rising, but she knew her brother loved her, and she wouldn't believe any differently no matter what was said. So, she began trying to pry Rachelle's hand off her arm. It was proving to be difficult because Rachelle had quite the grip for a small woman.

The pain was becoming worse, almost unbearable, so she tugged harder at Rachelle's hand as she muttered, "I will not be leaving, but you will be if I have anything to say about it. Now, let me go!"

"No, I won't let you go until you agree to leave," Rachelle informed her. "I'll drag you out of here by your hair if I have to, but you will be leaving..." Suddenly, she stiffened and gave a hard shiver. "Who turned up the air conditioning? It's so cold in here suddenly."

Andrina stopped her struggling to stare at the now shivering woman. *Why is she cold? I'm not cold, which must mean Thanatos is close. It must be him because he said people feel cold when he's around.* She felt like giggling and almost did. *Oh, Rachelle, if only it were just the air conditioning, but it's not. You are about to meet my man, the cause of your chill, and he is not going to be happy with you putting your hands on me in anger.*

After a quick glance around, she spotted Thanatos. Due to his height, he wasn't hard to find. A happy feeling bubbled up inside her as she gazed at him.

Raising her free hand in the air, she waved and called out, "Crusher!"

Thanatos moved quickly toward Andrina, almost shoving the crowd out of his way as he went. He had a look of extreme anger on his face, eyebrows pulled together, his jaw taut, and his lips pursed in a hard line. He was glaring at the hand Rachelle still had on Andrina's arm. Finally, reaching them, he growled, "If you wish to keep your hand, you will remove it from Andrina's arm."

Rachelle straightened, and with her nose in the air, she asked, "Who do you think you are?"

"It doesn't matter who I am," Thanatos answered.

"And you have no right to tell me what to do or any right to threaten me."

"I have many rights when it comes to Andrina, who you still have your hand on." Thanatos stepped closer. He watched as the girl shivered almost violently at his closeness, but he couldn't find it in himself to care. "What you need to think carefully about is how I can be a genuinely nice man if you do what I asked."

The girl rolled her eyes which only made his anger burn hotter.

"Or I can be your worst nightmare. Take your pick," Thanatos finished with a low growl.

"His name is Skull Crusher, and he's *my* fiancé," Andrina informed Rachelle with a grin.

Rachelle snorted as she said, "Skull Crusher. What kind of a name is that?"

Thanatos ignored Rachelle, as did Andrina, who asked, "I don't suppose you saw my brother anywhere, did you?"

Thanatos shook his head as he divulged, "He was not who I was searching for."

"Drat, I need that boy," Andrina muttered.

"Why?" Thanatos asked, curious. He was more than capable of getting rid of the girl if that was what his woman wanted.

"This… person here says she's my brother's fiancée, but I've never met her or even heard of her until tonight. Kristos never said anything about having a girlfriend to me. I mean, he has a right to his privacy, but he always tells me when he had a new girl in his life, which isn't often." Andrina sighed. "A fiancée, though? I would think that would have been important enough to mention. I would think he would have been shouting it to the world."

"You know your brother better than I do," Thanatos said calmly. "Which leads me to think she is lying."

Rachelle narrowed her eyes at Andrina as she loudly proclaimed, "I am not lying. I'm his fiancée!"

Andrina grimaced and let out a soft sound of pain. The pained whimper reminded Thanatos that Rachelle still had a hold on Andrina's arm. So, he grabbed hold of Rachelle's wrist and squeezed.

Rachelle cried out, letting go of Andrina's arm as she loudly asked, "Why did you do that? It feels as if you broke my wrist!"

"I told you to let her go earlier in a nice way, yet you did not let go," Thanatos growled out his answer to Rachelle before letting go of her arm. Taking Andrina into his arms, he gently rubbed over the gouges on her arm. He frowned, seeing how the woman's nails had dug in, almost breaking the skin. Bringing Andrina's arm up, he gently kissed the wounds, wishing he could take them from her.

"Andrina!"

Thanatos' head came up at the shout.

Kristos was making his way through the crowd, a worried frown on his face.

Hades and Irina were right behind him.

"There you are!" Kristos exclaimed as he came to a stop in front of them. "Your boyfriend's friends came to find me because they said you were in trouble."

"I am. I mean, I was, but Crusher came and rescued me," Andrina informed Kristos. Then, with her brows knitted in confusion, she asked, "How did they even know who you were? They've never met you."

Irina, who had made it to them by then, laughed. Waving a hand toward Kristos, she said, "Honey, please, notice the boy's face. It is the exact replica of yours."

"I don't look like her," Kristos muttered indignantly. "She's a girl, and I am all man."

Thanatos chuckled.

Irina huffed softly. "What I mean is, he's a *male* version of you, Andrina."

"That's a little better," Kristos interrupted to say.

Andrina rolled her eyes. "Kristos, you know what she meant, so stop being childish."

"So, how could we not know who he was?" Irina finally finished.

Hades spoke up, saying, "Skull was like an angry bull, shoving through the crowd. So, I thought you might need your family. Your mother is somewhere behind us, we met her along the way, and Irina mentioned you might need her. She's a bit more polite than the rest of us are, though, and said she would be along in a moment. I'm guessing she wished to finish the conversation she was having with some gaudily dressed woman."

"Be polite, Doom," Irina scolded.

"Just telling it as I see it," Hades informed his wife with a shrug.

Thanatos shook his head at Hades but turned his attention back to Andrina when she laughed. When she leaned into him, he hugged her close and began to run his hand up and down her arm gently.

"Yes, Mom is very polite. The flamboyantly dressed woman she was talking to was probably Mrs. Jordan, who has more money than fashion sense." Pulling away from him slightly, Andrina focused on her brother, pointing a finger at him as she demanded, "Kristos, you need to explain yourself."

"What am I explaining to you exactly?" Kristos asked.

"Explain to me why you never told me you have a fiancée. Who, it would seem, already hates me?"

"Fiancée? What are you talking about?" Kristos sputtered. "I don't have…"

"She said that's who she was," Andrina declared, cutting her brother off. She tilted her head to the side, indicating the woman who stood next to her. She then raised an enquiring eyebrow at her brother.

When all eyes turned Rachelle's way, she slowly began to back away as if she were getting ready to flee the scene.

However, before Rachelle could move another inch, Thanatos reached out his arm and grabbed her.

With a tight grip, he held her in place as he growled, "I think you need to stay right where you are. You have a lot to explain."

Rachelle stared at the floor, not speaking. Everyone stared at her as if waiting for her to explain herself.

When she didn't, Andrina stated, "This woman, she said her name is Rachelle, accosted me earlier as I was leaving the snack table and dragged me over to this dark corner." She was once more focusing on Kristos but was interrupted by the appearance of her mother.

"What is going on here?" Mrs. Dukakis asked as she came to a stop next to Kristos.

"That's what we're about to find out," Irina answered as she gave Mrs. Dukakis a sweet smile. "Andrina was just telling us how this girl," she pointed at Rachelle, "pulled her from the midst of the party to this corner."

"She grabbed me out of nowhere, Mom. Then she dragged me off over here and proceeded to tell me I needed to leave," Andrina continued. Taking a deep breath, she let it out slowly, blowing the short hairs from her forehead.

Thanatos rubbed her back gently, encouraging her.

"Kristos, she told me she was your fiancée. Well,

her exact words were that she *would be* your fiancée because she *knows* you're going to propose to her after the party tonight."

"Does she have the gift of prophecy like Apollo?" Hades questioned.

Thanatos snickered. "She seemingly believes she does, but by Kristos's reaction at being informed he has a fiancée, I don't think she got it right."

"Crusher," Andrina said with a soft laugh.

"Just saying it like it is, darling. Please, continue with your story," Thanatos murmured.

"Anyway, Rachelle was also notably clear in telling me that I wasn't wanted here and was threatening to throw me out of my party, bodily if she had to," Andrina concluded.

Mrs. Dukakis blinked, staring at Rachelle as if she weren't sure what to think of her. She finally turned her confused gaze to Kristos, asking, "Son, is this true? Were you planning to ask this girl to marry you?"

"No, I'm not planning to marry her, Mother!" Kristos proclaimed loudly. Stepping closer to his sister, he held out his hands and took hers. "Andrina, I just met her tonight and barely know her. I would have told you if I had a girl, I always do."

All the yelling had drawn a crowd. Kristos, his face red with his anger, ignored them as he continued to talk.

"She's the sister to one of the guys I met six months or so ago. He and I became close friends because he's in the same business as me. He told me a couple of days ago that his sister was in town visiting, and I told him he could bring her along. I'd never met her, but I remember him saying her name was Rachelle. I don't know what would give her the idea I'd ever ask her to marry me. All I did was greet her just as I greeted everyone else."

Everyone turned their attention to Rachelle. They might not have been asking, but their questions were straightforward. Why would she say such things, and why would she do this?

A few of the girls in the crowd began to giggle and whisper about what they were hearing. The girls stopped, though, with fear on their faces when Thanatos and Hades turned to glare at them. They quickly left as if deciding the drama they'd been watching wasn't worth it.

"We're waiting for an explanation, girl," Thanatos growled.

Rachelle shivered, whether from fear or cold, Thanatos didn't know. But she finally answered, "I knew if he just took time to know me, he'd like me. I'd seen him around before, so I know he's a good man and would make an excellent husband. I also heard a lot of the girls and a few guys talking about Andrina tonight. I realized that very few of the people here think much of her from what they were saying. I decided I'd probably be doing everyone a favor if I made her leave."

Both Kristos and Mrs. Dukakis stared at the girl, their eyes wide in disbelief. Thanatos shook his head in disgust. The girl was an idiot admitting such a thing to Andrina's family and friends. She could even lose her status with Kristos's friends for her stunt because of it.

Rachelle shivered harder, glancing around as she rubbed her hands up and down her arms. "I wish someone would turn the air conditioning off. It is getting icy in here."

Feeling a bit guilty at seeing the girl shiver, Thanatos moved further away from her, taking Andrina with him. He couldn't take the cold away entirely, but he could lessen it by not standing so close.

Andrina glanced at Thanatos as she squeezed him around the waist. She then turned away when she heard her mom began to speak.

"Well, Rachelle, I'd have to say you are a strange one," Mrs. Dukakis murmured. "To think you believed you would wrangle my son into marriage after only meeting him once and then try to kick my daughter from her own party on top of it. Now, I believe you will be the one leaving, and I wish never to see you again. So, if you happen to see me in town, please go the other way."

Everyone watched as Rachelle left, almost at a run, her head bowed low.

Mrs. Dukakis returned her focus to Andrina. "Now, what is this I'm hearing about the guests speaking badly of you? Don't think for one minute I didn't catch that. I believe it's something I should have heard from you, Andrina, not a stranger."

Andrina buried her face in Thanatos' abs and sighed.

Thanatos knew she didn't want to have this conversation with her mom. He also knew enough about Rachel Dukakis to know she wouldn't let it drop until she knew everything.

"I believe I'd like an answer to that also," Kristos added as he crossed his arms over his chest.

Thanatos took in the sad expression Kristos had on his face, identical to the one now on Andrina's. Giving her a gentle squeeze of encouragement, he whispered, "I told you, you should have told them, darling."

"I know, and you were right." Andrina straightened up, squaring her shoulders as she turned and faced her family.

Thanatos, now behind her, placed his hand on her shoulder, lending her strength.

CHAPTER SIXTEEN

Breathing deeply, Andrina began, "I didn't want you to know. Even when Crusher encouraged me to say something, I hedged, but I know I should have already told you both. The truth is most of the people here don't like me. They don't think I'm pretty enough, slim enough, smart enough, or something like that. I never fit in well with this crowd, but I tried because I knew how much it meant to Kristos. Mostly, I ignore the whispers about me and avoid those who are the most vicious with it. I have a few friends here, and they know about the backstabbing talk that circulates at these parties and other social events like it. They all try to keep me happy and busy so that I don't hear most of it."

"Oh, Andrina," Kristos murmured as he moved close enough to pull her into his arms in a hug. "You are my sister and so much more important to me than any of these people here tonight. You know I would have told them to hit the road had I known…"

"I know you would have because you've done it before," Andrina interrupted him to say, "and that's why I said nothing. They are your friends, and you deserve friends. I don't want to be the one to take them away from you, causing you to resent me in the process."

"I wouldn't do that," Kristos argued. "If they can't see in you what I see in you, they aren't worth my time. You are a sweet and loving girl, and it would be anyone's pleasure to know you." He straightened, squaring his shoulders, and took a deep breath as he turned to say, "Mom, I believe this party is over. Let us send everyone home except our special guests and Andrina's friends."

Mrs. Dukakis, who had tears in her eyes, smiled and agreed, "Excellent idea. I'll make the announcement. You round up Andrina's friends. I think I saw them earlier over at the snack table."

Kristos nodded and headed off, telling people as he went that it was time to leave.

Mrs. Dukakis turned to study Andrina and sighed sadly before saying, "I'm sorry I never saw how miserable these parties made you, Andrina. I also want you to know that I believe you have a smart young man there. The two of you have opened my eyes up to how much he sincerely cares for you." She glanced over at Thanatos as she added, "Take good care of her; she deserves only the best."

"I plan to give her exactly that," Thanatos informed his soon-to-be mother-in-law. "That is why I wish to ask you for your blessing to marry her."

Mrs. Dukakis's eyes widened before she gave a soft laugh, asking, "How did I not see that coming? Well, it appears as if I need to be more observant, but yes, you have my blessing."

Thanatos turned toward Andrina as he dropped to one knee and said, "Andrina, *glyké mou peirasmé,* my sweet temptation, this isn't exactly how I planned this, but will you marry me?"

Andrina laughed as she dropped to her knees in front of him. Pulling him into a tight hug, she exclaimed, "Yes! Oh, yes, I will marry you."

Thanatos softly chuckled as he pulled a ring from his pocket and placed it on her hand. He kissed the back of her hand lightly before standing and pulling her to her feet. "Perhaps we should take the bad memories of this party and make them perfect."

"Perfect?" Andrina asked, "How do you plan to do that?"

"By inviting me to join the party, of course," a voice from behind her said.

Andrina swiftly turned around and stared at the man behind her. It was Eros, dressed in a fancy tuxedo with a red vest and bowtie. He had a big grin on his face and held a flower bouquet in his hand.

Eros handed the flowers to her as he gave a slight bow, saying, "Can't break the tradition, I will be officiating this marriage."

Andrina's eyes widened as a few more men and women came to stand behind Eros. "Um, what are all of you doing here?"

"That's what I'd like to know," Kristos said as he came to stand next to Andrina. "Seriously, who are all you people, and how did you practically appear out of thin air?"

"Kristos, Mrs. Dukakis, I'd like you to meet the rest of the Steel Chariots, MC," Thanatos said. He began to point as he gave names, "Tank, and his wife Queen; Mad Dog, and his ol' lady Cathy; Doom, and his ol' lady Irina; Shark, Brewer, Prophet, Vixen, and Claws. I'm sure you've already figured out that the last guy is my twin brother, Hypnos."

"I, of course, am Crossbow," Eros murmured, giving a slight wave. "I have married Mad Dog and Doom, and now I am here to wed Skull and Andrina with all of you as witnesses."

A squeal split the air as the tiny blonde woman pushed her way through the crowd to throw herself at

Andrina, chattering excitedly. "Married! Oh, honey, I am so happy for you!"

Andrina laughed and put her arms around the woman as she told her, "Thank you, Sarah. I didn't exactly plan to tell you I had a fiancé at my birthday party, much less get married during it, but I guess it works."

Sarah, who was even shorter than Andrina, narrowed her eyes into slits as she tilted her head up to focus on Thanatos. "So, you must be the biker, Crusher, that Andrina has been gushing over for weeks now."

Thanatos nodded.

"You may be big, but the girls and I together could, and would, take you down if you were ever to hurt Andrina. She is a lovely girl, inside and out, and deserves only the best in this life," Sarah said.

"I plan to give her exactly that," Thanatos informed her as he pulled Andrina back into his arms. "She started as a sweet temptation that drew me in and grew to be someone who made me want to be more than what I was. I was walking, alone, in the darkness that pulled at me until I was a shell. Andrina came into my life and lit up that darkness because she saw the man in me, not just the darkness that dwells within. She is my light."

All the women awed at his words.

Hades let out a snort, saying, "Enough of the sappy mush, Skull. It is most unbecoming for a man to go on like that."

"Oh, hush you," Irina scolded as she tapped Hades' chest. "He's getting married, and a man has a right to be a bit mushy when he's fixing to be married."

"More like leg-shackled," Prophet muttered, only to put his hands up in surrender when everyone turned to glare at him.

Eros cleared his throat and said, "Well, shall we get started?"

"Wait! Who said there would be a wedding right now?" Kristos almost hollered out the question. "I know I said I was okay with my sister dating a biker, but I never…"

Mrs. Dukakis cut Kristos off when she took hold of his arm and gently said, "Enough, Kristos. She loves him, and he loves her; let them be happy. I loved your father, and he was taken from me so quickly because bad things in life happen, and we can't stop them. Let your sister be happy in the now because none of us know the future."

Andrina stared at her mother with tears in her eyes before she threw herself into her arms. She cried, "I love you, Mom!"

"And I love you," Mom answered with a slight

laugh. "Now, while your brother is quiet, let's get you married."

Andrina wiped her tears and laughed before saying, "Yeah, it won't last long, I'm sure." Turning, she took Thanatos' hands in hers as she said, "Okay, Crossbow, I'm ready to marry, my love, now."

"Dearly beloved, we are gathered here tonight to join the hearts and lives of these two lovebirds in matrimony..." Eros began.

Andrina barely heard the words, her eyes locked on Thanatos and the love she saw in his eyes. Soon, however, the "I do's" was said, and everyone was congratulating them.

Well, most everyone, Apollo, was still pouting in the corner with a cup in his hand, but she figured he'd get over it eventually. All he truly needed was a good woman of his own.

Kristos had finally given in and given her a big hug telling her how much he loved her, and he wanted her to be happy. She knew that, but sometimes it was nice to hear.

Tank narrowed his eyes and seemed to think about speaking, but with all the mortals around, she knew he didn't dare, and she found it funny. He looked as if he were about to choke, his face flushing every so often as he opened his mouth only to close it again when Hera elbowed him.

The rest all seemed to be having a good time, though, dancing and laughing. Andrina had even seen Kristos dancing with Artemis. Right now, Andrina was standing in a darkened corner, watching the interactions of the gods and the mortals. Thanatos had slipped out a few moments earlier because a spirit had been ready to leave its body. He'd told her he wouldn't be gone long, but she didn't want anyone to realize he was gone and ask questions she couldn't answer.

"So, Death himself was next to fall into the arms of fated love," a man whispered in Greek.

Andrina, startled, slightly jumped as she whipped her head around. Standing next to her was Dionysus. She noticed he had a bottle of whiskey in his hand and wondered where he'd gotten it because she knew it wasn't on the refreshment table here. Although she supposed it didn't matter in the grand scheme of things. What did matter was why he was standing next to her and rambling about fated love.

In Greek, she answered, "Yes, I suppose he was."

"It gives the rest of us poor saps the idea that the likelihood of us finding love isn't so farfetched after all," Dionysus continued. "It was quite a surprise when Hades and Ares succumbed to love. But when it happened to Thanatos, that shocked me, which was a shock in itself because very little phases me anymore." He took a swig of his whiskey as he gave her a wink.

239

"I've lived so long I thought I'd seen it all, or at least I thought I had."

"Do you wish to find love?" Andrina asked. She turned sideways, leaning a shoulder against the wall as she gave him her full attention.

"I had love once, the perfect love," Dionysus informed her after taking another swallow of his whiskey. His face was full of sadness and harsh lines as he stared at the dancers. "I lost her, though, when death took her, and I don't think I ever fully recovered. However, if love were to find me, I wouldn't turn it down."

Andrina patted his arm gently. When he turned his head toward her, she smiled. "Then I wish you the best."

"Wish him the best in what?" Thanatos asked as he joined them.

Andrina answered, "In finding what we have, love."

Thanatos smiled and murmured, "Love, the best thing I've found. Let me take you home now and show you the physical side of that love."

Andrina's face heated.

Dionysus laughed and walked away, slightly swaying as he said, "Enjoy yourselves, kids. The marriage bed is the best part of marriage.

Andrina watched until Dionysus was out of sight.

Giving Thanatos her full attention, she softly said, "I'd like that."

Thanatos kissed her, and they left the room in a cloud of grayish smoke.

When Thanatos pulled away from kissing her, Andrina realized they were no longer standing in the hotel ballroom. Swiveling her head, left then right, she saw they were in a bedroom.

"This is my room; I know you didn't see much of it when you were here before," Thanatos said, answering her unspoken question. "I thought about taking you to my home in the Underworld, but I thought you would be more comfortable here, at least for now."

Andrina smiled at him as she wrapped her arms around him, saying, "I would like to see your home in the Underworld, but for now, here is good. Hopefully, Kristos won't come hunting for me tomorrow since he knows where you live."

Thanatos ran his fingers through her hair, scattering hairpins as he went, saying, "He might try, but I believe your mother will stop him. If he does slip by her, I'm sure Hypnos will catch him and send him on his way."

"You mean to put him to sleep, don't you?" Andrina

murmured, a bit breathless now as his hands began to unzip her dress.

"Mm… perhaps, but enough talking now," Thanatos murmured, his dark eyes hooded as he pushed her dress from her shoulder. "I have waited for a very long time to give in to the temptation that is now my wife."

A shiver went through her as she felt his hand on her bare skin. She moaned as he cupped her breast, giving it a light squeeze, before she asked, "How is this fair? I'm almost naked, and you're still fully dressed."

As soon as the words were out of her mouth, his jacket, vest, and shirt were gone. A move that left his chest bare for her viewing pleasure.

"Oh, my, I need to be able to do that," she whispered as she ran her fingers over his tone chest. She lightly gripped his chest hair, giving it a slight tug, and listened to him moan in appreciation.

"When I make you immortal like myself, you will be able to," Thanatos enlightened her.

"Mm… I like that idea, but right now, I want us both naked and in your bed," Andrina commanded. "You are much too tall for me to do all the things I want to do."

Thanatos grinned and quickly removed the rest of his clothes and hers before picking her up. He lay her gently on the bed before joining her. While hovering over her, he leaned in to ravish her mouth, letting his hand roam her body. He learned every dip and curve, moaning at the feel of her soft skin against his.

It has been a shockingly long time since I've been this close to a woman, and it feels so good.

"Thanatos," she whimpered as his hand moved over her hip.

"I know, darling, it feels good, so good," he murmured before nipping at her ear.

"I want to feel you, all of you," she told him, her eyes opening to gaze into his as he lifted his head. "I never have…"

"I know," he told her. "In my lifetime, I will admit to having had a few women to scratch the itch, but very few because of the way I scare most. With you, though, I feel it will be so much more than just an act. With you, it will be lovemaking, and that makes me so incredibly happy."

Andrina smiled as she lifted her head so she could kiss him. As she did, she moved one hand down his chest, lower until she came to his manhood. She inhaled sharply at the size of him but didn't fear it, knowing they would fit perfectly together. With all of her heart, Andrina believed Thanatos was hers. She sighed as he broke the kiss and wrapped her hand around him, feeling the warm skin of his shaft. It was like steel encased in velvet, and it pulsed with life in her hand.

"Ah, darling, if you aren't careful, this will be over before it starts," Thanatos murmured.

His mouth slowly made its way over her chest, leaving behind wet kisses. His hand gently removed hers and placed it on his shoulder. He then sucked one nipple into his mouth, lapping at it with his tongue.

"Mm… sorry." She whimpered as his hand moved between her legs. She cried, her hips rising as his fingers moved through her damp folds, finding the bundle of nerves that set her on fire as he moved his thumb over it. She begged, "I want you, Thanatos, so bad do I want you. I want to feel you inside me, now, please."

"Wait, darling, let me…"

"No, no, more waiting," she cried. "I've waited so long for you, don't make me wait longer."

Thanatos wanted to give in to her pleas because he wanted her just as desperately. However, he knew if he didn't prepare her, he would hurt her because of his size. So, ignoring her begging, he kissed her once more. He then slipped his tongue into her mouth as his fingers moved through her folds to slip inside her.

She grabbed at his hair, tugging as her hips bucked. When he broke the kiss, she let out a long, keening whimper as he once more sucked on her breast. His fingers continued to slide in and out, her hips moving in rhythm with them.

When he felt she was ready for him, he lifted his head from her breast to demand, "Spread your legs for me, darling, let me love you completely now."

"Yes," Andrina agreed. Spreading her legs for Thanatos, she continued to move restlessly, needing fulfillment.

Thanatos moved over her, his wide hips fitting perfectly into the space between her thighs. He leaned in to kiss her, nibbling her lower lip slightly as she continued to make her seductive sounds. He felt her body tremble in anticipation of what was to come as her eyes met and held his. His own body was also trembling with need. He needed to pleasure her, but he wanted her body ready for him so he wouldn't hurt her.

"Are you ready?"

"I am so ready for you, my love," she agreed.

Lowering his hips in a smooth move, he penetrated her folds, sliding through her wetness and feeling her heat. He groaned at how good she felt and felt his shaft swell even more. She whimpered under him, and he stopped, opening his eyes to peer down at her. Seeing only passion on her face, not pain, he continued to push deeper, lowering his head to capture her lips with his. He met resistance and pulled back.

Andrina gripped his shoulders, her head thrashing as she whimpered, "No, don't stop now, Thanatos, please, don't stop."

So, with a deep breath, he thrust, plunging deep and breaking through the barrier of her innocence.

Andrina gave a cry, her body stiffening even as she tightened around him.

Thanatos held his breath momentarily, his body perfectly still as he waited. When he felt her body relax, he relaxed also and began to thrust once more. Soon, the only sounds in the room were their moans and grunts of passion, along with the sound of flesh against flesh. Time meant nothing as they made love until they both had found satisfaction and release.

Coming down of the cloud of passion, Thanatos observed the flushed face of his new bride and smiled. Oh, how he loved this woman, his temptation, his wife.

Speaking in Greek, he told her, "I love you, my sweet temptation. You are now my everything, my friend, my lover, my wife. Hopefully, in the not-too-distant future, you will also be the mother of my children."

Andrina's eyes widened as she giggled. "Maybe sooner than you think since you forgot to put a sock on it."

Thanatos felt his own eyes widen at the realization of what he had done.

"It's okay. I know I'm young, but considering how long we will live, we'll still have plenty of time for just the two of us," Andrina reassured him as she brushed her hand over the five o'clock shadow along his jawline. "I love you, Thanatos, and I want to have many babies with you."

Moving over to her side, he pulled the covers up over them before he pulled her close. Sighing with content, he heard her give one of her own and smiled. The darkness of the bedroom no longer felt like a weight holding him down. He had found his light in this woman he now called his wife, and he couldn't be happier.

"Thanatos, which one of the gods do you think will tumble into the hands of the fates and fall in love next?" Andrina asked in a sleepy voice.

"I don't know, but whoever it is will be a lucky man. Just like I am right now."

"And the woman will be just as lucky as me." She yawned loudly before sighing and snuggling into his side, one hand under his hip.

"Sleep now, *glyké mou peirasmé*," Thanatos suggested. "For I have plans to ravish you again, soon."

"Mm…" Andrina sighed, "I love it when you call me

your sweet temptation, and I like the idea of you ravishing me too."

Then, his temptation fell fast asleep in his arms where Thanatos knew the *Moirai* meant for her to be all along.

The End

OTHER BOOKS BY E. ADAMSON

STEEL CHARIOT'S, MC
Hades: His Jewel {Book One}
Ares: His Warrior {Book Two}

E. ADAMSON
romance author

I live in a small town in Alabama with my husband,
our two girls, and a cat named Minecraft. In my free
time, you can usually find me furiously writing on
something new, daydreaming about what to write
next, or reading someone else's book.

Be Sure to check out E. Adamson

Facebook:

Bookbub:

Goodreads:

Amazon:

Printed in Great Britain
by Amazon

72745933R00153